"I'm not offering you a job—more a *role*... You could think of it as a temporary contract. Say six months?"

"Is it a promotion?" Tilda was in no position to dismiss it out of hand, something with more flexibility would give her time to look for something more appropriate...but Greece? No, that was *too* crazy...too far away. Though maybe far away was good?

"That kind of depends on your viewpoint."

She muted the dialogue in her head and decided there was no harm hearing him out. "It's real?" Her history of being around Ezio told her it was not likely to be an invention, but she had to check. "I'm not a charity case."

He sighed. "I'm suggesting that we spend the next six months as husband and wife, so basically six months in Greece. Long enough to make people think we gave it a try and you found me impossible to live with."

Shock collided with disbelief in her spinning head. Her brain went into shock and closed down.

Kim Lawrence lives on a farm in Anglesey with her university-lecturer husband, assorted pets who arrived as strays and never left, and sometimes one or both of her boomerang sons. When she's not writing, she loves to be outdoors gardening or walking on one of the beaches for which the island is famous—along with being the place where Prince William and Catherine made their first home!

Books by Kim Lawrence

Harlequin Presents

A Wedding at the Italian's Demand
A Passionate Night with the Greek

Jet-set Billionaires

Innocent in the Sicilian's Palazzo

Spanish Secret Heirs

The Spaniard's Surprise Love-Child
Claiming His Unknown Son

A Ring from a Billionaire

Waking Up in His Royal Bed
The Italian's Bride on Paper

Visit the Author Profile page
at Harlequin.com for more titles.

CLAIMED BY HER
GREEK BOSS

CHAPTER ONE

THE GLASS DOORS swished open silently.

Tilda Raven shook the raindrops from her rich brown hair, the damp, messy waves spilling down her back almost to her waist today rather than constrained in the usual sensible, sleek, fat ponytail on her nape.

Tilda didn't pause. She was a woman on a mission, a mission interrupted by a security guard who blocked her way with his bulk.

'Do you have an appoint…?' The smartly suited man did a comical double-take. 'Oh, sorry, Miss Raven, I didn't recognise you.'

Tilda smothered her impatience and out of deeply engrained politeness forced her lips into a smile of acknowledgement that didn't touch the wide green eyes hidden behind the rain-spattered, pink-tinted lenses of the unflattering heavy-framed glasses that covered a lot of her small heart-shaped face.

Her eyes strayed beyond the uniformed figure to the art deco clock on the wall above the sleek reception desk. Yes, she could still make it back for three if... Her rounded jaw firmed. There was no *if* about it; she *was* going to be back for three—non-negotiable.

It wasn't as if he could try to lock her in!

Although she could easily imagine her terminally selfish boss doing just that, if he could have got away with it.

How would he take it?

'Not well' was pretty much a given.

At that moment the coward's way out was looking very appealing—she had been tempted—but she owed him an explanation in person if nothing else. Her decision was made and there was no going back—though Ezio could be very persuasive.

She was pretty sure that he wouldn't be wishing her well, but she was prepared for him to kick off.

She didn't care. For once this wasn't about her brilliant billionaire boss; this was about her brother, Sam.

Sam was her priority.

Better late than never.

Tilda felt a kick of guilt as an image of her teenage brother's scared eyes above an oxygen mask flashed into her head... Her hand went to her throat, her chest tightened, the sound of her heartbeat filled her ears and she fought for breath the way Sam had... *He's fine now...he's fine now...* She repeated the mantra, her head fighting free of the panic.

Sam *was* fine. You'd never know, seeing him sit-

KIM LAWRENCE   9

ting glued to a computer screen playing a game, that last night he'd been blue-lighted to hospital. If anything did happen, Mrs Lowther—the elderly neighbour who had known them since they were children—was sitting with him, much to Sam's disgust.

She realised that the security guard was talking to her and she hadn't heard a word he had said.

'Sorry, James.' She interrupted him mid-flow. 'I'm... I'll catch up later.' She threw the suitably vague promise over her shoulder, knowing it was a lie as she hurried across the space designed to give anyone visiting the iconic Angelos Building for the first time a serious *wow* moment.

Tilda still got a little frisson of pleasure when she walked in, but today she was not interested in the eclectic art, the modern sculptures, the polished concrete floor or the clever use of light. Her eyes went again to the stylised art deco clock behind the elegant reception desk staffed by an equally elegant team of reception staff. It wasn't actually morning, but even though that didn't matter any longer she found herself quickening her pace.

A bit like a condemned person being in a hurry for their last meal... The image drew a frown. She was not condemned—this was her choice—she just hated being late.

It was a lucky hang-up, given who her boss was, that she was an uber-punctual person, because tardiness and being kept waiting were on the list of things that wound up Ezio Angelos. The list was not short and it included excuses.

Not that she was about to offer any today. The only thing she planned to offer was her resignation. Not because she'd had a better offer—well, not recently, anyhow—or because she disliked her job, because she didn't, despite the fact that her boss ticked a lot of boxes on Tilda's own list of undesirable qualities in a man.

Many people were willing to overlook those qualities because they came wrapped up in some pretty marvellous packaging. Had she been the sort of female that went for smouldering, lean beefcake with the odd billion in his personal account, she might have too. But Tilda had higher standards. And being the owner of ridiculously long eyelashes, sybaritic cheekbones and a carnal mouth that should have carried a health warning did not, to her mind, make it all right for him to be arrogant.

And he was arrogance on steroids!

He also possessed the empathy of a flint, a ruthless streak a mile wide and as for beautiful women… He went through more of them than he did disposable razors—and her Greek boss, who possessed a carved jaw and lean cheeks that were dusted with a shadow before midday, went through quite a few of those.

Despite all these faults, Ezio, who had made his fortune in AI, was a pretty good boss. He was demanding, sure, but fair, not patronising and the work was *never boring*. Breathless, sure, but *not* boring.

The man was an intellectual adrenaline-junkie who considered the word 'impossible' a challenge. It could be pretty exhausting just trying to keep up with him. Tilda usually failed but she loved the buzz she got trying.

Also, she had a level of autonomy that she could not imagine being granted elsewhere. And in Tilda's eyes it really went in his favour that there were never any of the sort of inappropriate remarks or looks that had made her feel uncomfortable in her previous jobs. Equally importantly, he had not once suggested she looked too young to be taken seriously. She was sure this was in part thanks to the glasses her twenty-twenty vision didn't need, a piece of stage dressing that in her estimation added a good five years to her baby-faced twenty-six. They were an inspired prop, even if she acknowledged she shouldn't have to prove her seriousness anyway.

A flicker of regret slid across her face. She would miss her job. Also, if she was honest, she would miss the expression on people's faces when she casually threw into the conversation she was Ezio Angelos's PA… Yes, *the* Ezio Angelos…

Levering her back from the wall of the lift as it arrived at the top floor, she felt a stab of guilt at the selfish and shallow thought. She straightened her slender shoulders and reflected wryly that there might be no need to resign. Maybe she was already sacked. Ezio was not exactly renowned for his patience and she was *extremely* late.

She glanced quickly at her phone just to check for messages from Sam but there weren't any. She was only partially soothed. There had been no messages from him last night when she'd thought he was at his chess club. It turned out that he'd actually been in the local hospital A&E department.

And she had only found out thanks to the owner of a corner shop who had been incredibly kind—considering Sam had just tried to shoplift a can of beer from him—and had gone in the ambulance with the would-be thief after Sam's efforts to be accepted by the *cool* older school kids had triggered an asthma attack. The worst one he'd had in years.

If it hadn't been for the actions of the shop keeper in being so quick to call an ambulance, and who wasn't pressing charges, Sam's future might be looking very different today.

She shuddered. He might not have a future!

They owed that man a lot... Tilda could have kissed him...she actually had. His well-meant advice on parenting was a very small price to pay for his kindness. *And, let's face it,* she thought, sketching a bleak, self-condemnatory grimace, *I need it!*

The lift opened directly into a large room that was dominated by her own desk. She could see the shadow of her assistant distorted through the thick glass partition. Even now, after four years, the novelty of having an assistant and not being *the* assistant hit her some days.

She reached the open door, beyond which lay the

spectacular architectural award-winning office with
the glass wall along with its outward-projecting glass-
floored section that only someone with a head for
heights would venture near—Tilda hadn't.

In her own head, Tilda had never thought of it as
an office. Instead *lair* had always seemed a more appropriate description, fit for the sleek predator her
boss of four years was.

She took a deep breath, stepped inside the *lair*
and turned to close the door just as Rowena emerged
from her office alcove, desperately mouthing, '*He's
in a vile mood*,' as she dramatically mimed a cut-
ting motion across her throat in a well-meant dramatic warning.

Tilda didn't need the warning. Even without Tilda
seeing his face, Ezio's clenched body language said
it all. His loose-limbed body was rigid and she could
almost see the quivering tension in his broad shoulders as he stood facing the glass wall, oblivious to
the dizziness of the drop visible beneath his feet, listening to the disembodied voice on speaker phone
that she immediately recognised belonged to Saul
Rutherford.

The image of the man frequently termed 'a silver
fox', a legend in his own life time, flashed into her
head. In his seventies, Saul still ran his successful
IT firm, niche rather than revolutionary these days,
but his name still carried clout.

'I would let my company go under before I would
let Baros get his claws into it.' Tilda could hear the

bubbling anger in the normally softly spoken man's shaking voice.

'There is no question of either of those eventualities coming to pass, is there, Saul?'

Nothing of the explosive quality he was exuding was evident in Ezio's measured response, which emerged cool and silky-smooth, giving no hint of the frustration she could see drawn on his lean, dark 'fallen angel' features as he swivelled round, looking exclusive and sleek in one of the gorgeously cut suits he habitually wore. He registered her presence with a narrowing of his black, dark-framed eyes—eyelashes like his were wasted on a man—and a sharp, stabbing motion of one long, elegant brown finger that she followed to the crumpled tabloid lying open on the desk.

Even before she saw the two-year-old, digitally altered photo, the fake headline above it drew a grimace. This represented a sharp escalation of the drip-drip of stories attributed to people close to the 'couple'.

Surely this was the moment for him to speak directly to Athena? Because ignoring her wasn't working... Maybe, she mused, it was the *ignoring* that was part of the problem.

Or maybe it was just revenge, spite or maybe...?

She gave her head a tiny shake and closed down the line of speculation.

It was hard to take on the new reality, which was that she was no longer totally invested in her boss's projects or problems. It was no longer her job to point out the options he didn't want to see and to quite often get her head bitten off for her trouble.

Focusing on the plusses somehow didn't make her feel any happier, but this wasn't about being happy; it was about being there for her brother.

Ezio was no longer her problem, but Athena Baros was his. Tilda was actually amazed this sort of situation didn't occur more often, considering the callous way Ezio dumped the women in his life, but generally they seemed remarkably un-resentful. Certainly, none had previously planted a series of false stories which left the impression that their romance had been rekindled.

Sources close to the socialite *influencer* Athena Baros denied it. She had maintained a loud silence but her enigmatic smile had set names trending. According to an online survey, nine out of ten people were convinced that not only were the beautiful pair secretly engaged, Athena was pregnant.

Tilda wondered if Ezio had read the same survey. Being sane, she hadn't asked. It wasn't that, as far as she could tell, he gave a damn how many articles were written about his love life—which was just as well, as when your name appeared regularly in the top five eligible bachelors on the market the stories were par for the course. But this was different because this time it wasn't personal, it was business, and when it came to business Ezio was never casual. Focused and ruthless, yes, but not casual.

He had invested a good deal of time and effort in the Rutherford deal. Tilda knew it was part of his vision for the future of Angelos Industries. And if her boss was invested, he expected her to be too, and that was the problem. While she'd been giving her all to her job, what had been left over for the really important things? Her priorities had got seriously skewed, but that was going to stop right here, right now.

She might not a be parent but she was the closest thing to a parent that Sam had now.

The self-recriminatory groove in her forehead smoothed out as she lifted her chin. Beating herself up over past mistakes would achieve nothing; her priorities had been redrawn. Ezio's billion-making deals did not even make the revised top hundred. She was about to focus all her energies on keeping her brother safe, stopping him from falling in with the wrong crowd and wrecking his life.

This had been a warning and she was heeding it.

'Even without us joining forces on this project, Rutherford has the respect of the industry and balance sheets to match. Of course, if you join us you will step into a different league...'

'You expect me to get into bed with you when you are in bed with Baros's daughter, that lying snake... He's been trying for years get his hands on my company.'

She watched as Ezio paused, no doubt swallowing an acid rejoinder on the tip of his tongue, and pressed a row of long fingers to his temple.

'Athena and I had a casual relationship several years ago.'

The muscle that was clenching and unclenching beside his mouth as he formed the words through bared white teeth held an unwilling fascination for Tilda, who knew how much the words must cost him.

She had learnt pretty soon after she'd come to work for him, first as an assistant to his assistant and then as his PA, that he never explained himself to anyone, and she could only imagine what being obliged to do so now must be doing to him.

Welcome to the real world, she thought, unable to summon a shred of sympathy for his dilemma in her present mindset. Ezio didn't realise how lucky he was... Oh, not because of his wealth or power—she didn't envy him that—but he didn't seem to possess a shred of self-doubt. He didn't pretend to believe in himself, he actually did.

'Baros is not involved, Saul, and never has been.' Nothing in Ezio's expressionless delivery suggested that he was starting to have doubts on this score himself.

Given the timing and the escalation, how could he discount the possibility that George Baros, Athena's father, was behind this somehow? Hell, the two old men had been playing a grudge match for the past fifty years...they certainly kept the animosity fresh.

Was Athena helping her father out using this non-romance as a way of killing off a deal that would benefit her father's old enemy?

Along with the most incredible legs, Athena did possess a rather twisted sense of humour, and no discernible conscience. That had not bothered him any more than the fact that he and the guy who'd replaced him in her bed had overlapped by several weeks... There had been no drama, no big romance, they had just drifted apart.

'Saul, I can—' The sound of the phone being slammed down in some distant office echoed around the silent room.

Tilda held her breath and fought the craziest urge to laugh... Someone had hung up on Ezio! A wicked part of her wanted to applaud.

The silence stretched until Ezio broke it by stringing together a volley of curses in his native tongue, with a few random languages thrown in.

'What does she hope to achieve by this?'

He dragged a hand through the dark hair that sprang from his broad, bronzed brow, and Tilda watched his eyes narrow to black glass slits, before he turned and adopted his previous pose, feet apart, rocking on his heels, spine straight, staring out at the panorama of the city far below.

This was the cue for Tilda to get on with something, but she wasn't in the mood to be tuned out.

Not today!

She was not in the mood to be dismissed.

She felt the outrage that she hadn't known was there tighten in her chest. She hadn't been late *once* in four years, and he hadn't even asked if there was a problem. But then it was always about Ezio, she thought, feeding the heated core of resentment.

'You seriously don't know why she's doing this?'

He spun back, pinning her with an incredulous, laser-like stare.

She didn't slink away into a corner. Instead she met his stare with one of her own, though it was hard to trade glares when her eyes were hidden behind the tinted lenses.

'Just thought you might like my input.' He was great at delivering sarcastic jabs, but she doubted he'd even recognise it when he was on the receiving end of one.

'Athena and I moved on two years ago.' About to turn away again, he paused when she spoke.

'*You* moved on…it's not actually the same thing.' Her disproval of his attitude to women was genuine; her sisterly solidarity with the other woman was more forced. On the handful of occasions she had encountered Athena Baros, the tall blonde had acted as though she'd been invisible. Her sweetness was reserved for people who were of use to her.

Tilda shrugged and bit back the apology on the tip of her tongue, reminding herself that, as a soon-to-be ex-employee, she was no longer obliged to polish his ego or say the right thing. 'Maybe she's trying to make you notice she's still alive,' she mused, half to herself, thinking, *good luck with that.* 'Just a thought,' she added, producing a faint half-smile.

His dark brows were knitted in a perplexed weave as his stare travelled the length of her petite, slim figure, moving from her face to her feet and back again as though he was seeing her for the first time.

'Athena does not connect sex with her emotions...' He realised that he had just come dangerously close to excusing himself to his PA, who was...late, which was a first, and...

If he'd been asked to describe Matilda Raven in one word, it would have been neat. She did not look neat, she looked...*different*, he decided, noting the heavy chunk of rich brown hair that fell against one cheek, the rest either tumbling down her back or stuck down the collar of a padded jacket that was fastened on the wrong buttons.

'You're late and...what the hell are you wearing?' He dismissed his own question without waiting for a response. What his PA chose to wear was of minor importance.

With a sharp shake of his dark head, he abruptly folded his long frame into the miracle of ergonomically designed blonde wood-and-metal chair behind the desk and directed his probing stare at the tips of his long, brown steepled fingers.

He heard her take a deep breath before she spoke. 'I'm sorry, I know this is a bad time, but I'm leaving.'

His eyes lifted as he expelled a long, sibilant sigh

of irritation and fought to keep a lid on his frustration. In four years, Matilda Raven had only taken time off for a root-canal filling and had been directly back at her desk, though he'd sent her home because he hadn't been able to understand a word she was saying. Now she was calling him an unfeeling monster and absenting herself just when her presence as a sounding board would be useful.

'How long do you need?' He didn't ask for reasons. He was assuming something worse than a root canal. To his mind, his staff's personal life was none of his business so long as it did not impact their efficiency during working hours. His distracted gaze slid from her face and, though he was not a person inclined to question the staring-you-in-the-face obvious, he heard himself ask, 'Are those *jeans*?'

Matilda's eyes drifted downwards. 'Yes, and for ever... I'm resigning.'

'You choose your moment.'

She shook her head, seeming bewildered by his calm reaction.

Ezio felt the muscles along his jawline quiver. This was not the moment for Matilda to start negotiating for a rise. 'Shall we cut the drama? How much do you want? Actually, can this wait until later? Or, better still, contact HR and tell them I've authorised a pay rise...you decide what you're worth. I need to find out if—'

'No!' she blurted.

The frown playing across his broad brow deepened, digging out the semi-permanent frown line that was developing between his dark brows. She planted her hands on her hips and glared at him, the two red circles on her cheeks emphasising she hadn't even applied the discreet make-up she normally wore to the office.

He had never seen his PA wear anything but black, normally an A-line tailored skirt teamed with a white blouse. There had been black trousers that had revealed details that the skirt had not, but in jeans that went double...possibly treble. Her legs were slim and disproportionally long for her diminutive height and her behind was... Clearing his throat, Ezio lifted his gaze, irritated it required an effort.

Admiration of feminine bottoms had its place in his life but not in his work place. He maintained a scrupulously clear-cut, unambiguous line between the personal and private and he expected his staff to do the same. Realistically, relationships developed, but when they did he expected that line between professional and personal to be observed.

It was perfectly possible to do so, just as it was possible to notice that his PA was good to look at, *despite* her efforts to disguise the fact, without dwelling on the fact she had a waist and one so slender he could have spanned it between his hands.

He met the eyes looking back at him, the colour indeterminate behind the pinkish-tinted lenses of a pair of owlish spectacles. Her fashion sense was unimportant to him; the important thing was he could always rely on her sharp brain, cool head, her calm practicality and her absolute, total discretion.

He clenched his teeth, then dug deep into his reserves of patience and smiled. 'Look, Matilda, shall we start this conversation again? Clearly you've had some issues this morning.' *Though not as bad as mine*, he thought, congratulating himself on being so tolerant.

Tilda pushed her glasses further up and folded her arms across her heaving chest. He wasn't listening, he wasn't *hearing*. 'The smile isn't going to do it.'

He looked bemused by the tart comment. 'And it's Tilda, not Matilda. Everyone else in the universe knows that!

'I thought Matilda was your name.'

'It is but that isn't the point—the point is, I'm resigning.'

'*Resigning?*'

She nodded, taking a tiny spurt of irrational pleasure from the stunned disbelief on his face. 'And you know something? You're making it so much easier because you're just…just…' She scanned his face and closed her lips against the unwise but honest addition that was on the tip of her tongue.

Best left unsaid but true. He *was* the most incredible-looking man on the planet, and the irony was he was probably too arrogant even to have noticed. His confidence had nothing to do with his amassed billions or his painfully perfect profile—it was as much part of him as his fingerprints.

Dragging a few shallow breaths, she tried to regain some sort of sanity, and failed when his gaze zeroed in on her face. Her stomach dipped dramatically. She had seen that look before, seen the perfect symmetry of his face harden to ice and watched the dangerous smile that left his eyes cold...the moment before he went in for the kill in the financial sense.

'Just...?' Ezio prompted, the chilly edge of his voice making it clear, if she hadn't already twigged, that his anger had shifted from the ex-lover who was putting his business deal at risk.

Her chin lifted as she embraced her antagonism. After all, they were things she had wanted to say for four years, so why not?

'An entitled, selfish...' She stopped and swallowed a sob that was trying to fight its way out of her chest.

'Oh, don't hold back, this is fascinating.'

'I shouldn't have said that... I have liked working for you, but that doesn't mean you're a...a *nice* person. I know you're going to say I was late and you didn't bawl me out, but that's only because you know I'll make up the hours. You haven't asked me what's wrong because, the fact is, you're not even vaguely interested, you're the most selfish, self-absorbed man I have ever met.'

'A monster, in fact.'

A beautiful monster!

'Possibly you should have remembered that fact before you opted for brutal honesty.' He pressed the intercom on his desk. 'Rowena, call Security and have them escort Miss Raven and her belongings from the building.'

Tilda lifted her chin. *So maybe not the best time to ask for a reference.*

There was a long silence and then, 'You can't sack someone because they are late.'

The unexpected support from the disembodied voice belonging to her shy, nervous assistant brought an emotional lump to Tilda's throat.

'Oh, it's OK, I want to go, Rowena,' she said, resisting the impulse to applaud her assistant. The last thing she needed was anything else on her conscience and she certainly did not want to be responsible for the brave young woman losing her job.

Ezio threw up his hands. 'What is this, "bring your protest placard to work" day?' he wondered, incensed, dragging a hand through his dark hair.

'It's fine,' Tilda inserted, not fooled by Ezio's languid tone. She could take his moods but poor Rowena got flustered every time he spoke to her. 'Don't worry, Rowena, call them. I could do with some help to carry my things.'

Her face was filled with haughty contempt when she turned back to Ezio. 'Actually, I am quite capable of leaving under my own steam, thank you.' Mid-stiff-backed turn, she caught sight of the discarded tabloid on the periphery of her vision and made a detour to pick it up. 'If you want to kill the story dead, you could always marry someone else—another of the rejects you treat like rubbish, maybe?'

The words hung there... Another time, the look of sheer disbelief on Ezio's handsome face would have made her laugh, but instead she felt a stinging tightness in her throat and a burning heat beneath her eyelids.

She would not cry.

Teeth clenched, she turned her defiant gaze back to Ezio and flung the paper back down on the desk, not realising that the jerky action had dislodged the plastic hospital identity bracelet she had shoved in her jeans pocket after Sam had torn it off in the taxi. It nose-dived an inch in front of her feet and, before she could retrieve it, Ezio came round from behind his desk and picked the tag up.

'What is this...?' Ezio's dark eyes went to her pale face...he realised for the first time just how pale. 'You have been in hospital?' The tightness in his chest stemmed from a surge of emotion that he felt no desire to examine. 'Why didn't you say so?' he growled out. In light of this information, a quick review confirmed he had acted badly, but how the hell was he to know if she didn't tell him?

'Why didn't you ask?' she countered, totally abandoning the polite office voice he was used to as she yelled, 'Not me, my... Samuel!' She stopped, clearly just one quivering syllable short of a sob, and bit her lip hard.

She held out her hand for the bracelet but, instead of handing it back, Ezio read the name on it.

'Who is *Samuel*…?'

She had a boyfriend?

CHAPTER TWO

'YOUR BOYFRIEND?'

'My brother.' She wasn't against the idea of a boyfriend but she wasn't actively looking for one. According to Rowena—who would have chatted constantly about her own boyfriend if Tilda didn't stop her—that was a mistake, because they didn't come knocking on your door. Also Tilda, apparently—again, according to Rowena—didn't put out *signals*, or at least not the right ones for men to know she was interested.

Maybe she set the bar too high. Her assistant had tentatively suggested this before dissolving into confusion as she'd hastily assured Tilda that she was really very pretty, and a very nice person, which was what counted. She probably wasn't so nice, because she had been amused to watch the younger girl tie herself in knots, offering reassurance that Tilda did not need.

The fact was, she honestly didn't care. Romance was the last thing on her mind and, as for sex, what you'd never had you never missed. The celibacy had been a conscious choice. She had decided early on in her guardianship that she wasn't going to disrupt her brother's life by having a stream of random men drift in and out of his life.

Love might be different, but for the life of her Tilda couldn't figure out how you were meant to know that attraction was something deeper. It made total sense that you had to kiss a lot of frogs.

She had a brother? Ezio felt some of the unaccountable antagonism that had climbed its way into his shoulders lessen.

Had he known she had a brother…?

Did he want to?

Annoyed at the scratch on his conscience, he handed her the plastic identity tag.

Tilda sniffed as she shoved it into one of her jacket's many pockets. 'I need to get home.'

'Your par—'

Big eyes behind her lenses flew to his face, and the memory of scanning her HR file in the past surfaced in his head. She had lost both her parents in a motorway smash; he must have read about the brother.

Was *that* why she had hadn't come to the job through the usual university route?

'So now you are his sole guardian?'

She nodded without looking at him.

'Was there no one else?'

'We are fine.' Her defensive prickles were on full show as she met his stare head-on. 'Sam is a good boy… He…he got in with the wrong crowd.'

'Ah…!' How many career criminal families said the same thing? He was thinking, quite a few.

Her chin snapped up as she fixed him with a glare, and behind the spectacles her eyes glittered dangerously. 'What does *that* mean?' she said, her tone daring him to say anything bad about her brother.

'Your brother is still in hospital?'

With no warning, the tears filled her eyes again. She blinked rapidly to disperse the warm moisture as her glasses steamed up. 'No, he's home now.'

'So it wasn't serious.'

'Serious,' she echoed, her nostrils flaring. 'I suppose it depends on what you call serious, but most people would think that an asthma attack that requires hospitalisation is serious. If he'd been alone… But he wasn't, luckily. I wasn't there because I was working late. I actually spend more time with you than my own brother and…' She gulped and stamped her foot for emphasis. 'And that ends here and now!'

'You need some time…?'

'I have all the time in the world. I'm sacked!'

'You resigned, as I recall.'

She paused. 'We'll be fine,' she said, more for her own benefit than his. 'Maybe I'll rent our house out and Sam and I could find a smaller rental somewhere cheaper… Cornwall, maybe?' she said, her expression lightening as she was struck by the option. 'We used to go there every year on holiday. It was quiet and Sam…' She stopped suddenly, pressing both hands to her mouth.

If she hadn't been projecting mute distress, Ezio would have pointed out the flaws in this plan. He would have pointed out that rental property was limited in Cornwall, where the popularity of the holiday hot spot had priced so many locals out of the property market, but she didn't look as though she could take even a gentle version of the truth.

A profound sense of helplessness crashed down on Tilda like a black cloud smothering her normally buoyant optimism. She simply couldn't see a way out that had a happy ending. There was just a series of brick walls blocking her way.

Their house was worth a lot and they owned it outright, which was lucky, because there wasn't much left of what little insurance there had been and she had set that aside for Sam's future. She hated the idea of selling the family home that held so many memories but recognised now that there might be no choice. But, even if they did move, it wouldn't matter where they went because Sam would always be the outsider, always trying to fit in, and for the life of her she didn't know how to help him.

'Take a sabbatical. Your job will be waiting.'

He looked as surprised as she felt at his words. She felt a sudden a glimmer of hope, along with a lot more wariness.

'Why are you being so nice?' There had to be a catch. 'And it doesn't matter, because I don't need a sabbatical, I need for ever!' Aware her voice had risen to a shrill level of panic, she made a conscious effort to lower it as she added, 'I can't work, you take too much, and...' The wobble was back but this time there was no way of stopping it morphing into a long wail of distress. In that moment it felt as though she would never be all right again... She was alone and she had broken the promise she made to her parents at the funeral that she would keep Sam safe.

The sound horrified her but it just went on and on.

Finally she made it stop, and rammed her hands across her mouth as though to retain the control that she was leaking from every pore. *Oh, God, just hold it together, you idiot.* To lose it like that in front of anyone was humiliating...but in front of Ezio it felt a million times worse.

She flashed a look towards the tall figure who had not moved a muscle during her meltdown.

Ezio watched her almost visibly unravelling—she looked *breakable.* He felt something he could not put a name to tighten in his chest. That awful wrenching, feral cry of anguish had stopped, though he could still hear it, *feel* it. She was still crying behind her hands; he could hear the muffled sobs.

Female tears did not normally affect him. In general he viewed them with cynical objectivity. He didn't have total immunity, but he was getting there.

Normally he simply removed himself from any situation that involved them but this was different. This was not a generic female, it was buttoned-up, tight *Matilda*. And that visceral sound…

'Perhaps it might be wise to talk to someone?' His mother swore by therapy, and said that she would not have been able to cope with her undemonstrative, dogmatic, cheating husband without it. Ezio thought that leaving him would have been a cheaper option.

Matilda's eyes lifted. She didn't make the mistake of interpreting the comment as an invitation to share with him, more a push towards the door, and she offered him a frigid little nod.

'Could Rowena call me a taxi, do you think?' she said quietly.

He knew there would be tears behind the misted lenses, and with no warning he found himself thinking of another office and another woman with tears in her eyes.

The roles on that occasion had been reversed. The woman in question that day had been *his* boss, his older, beautiful, charismatic and—as she had told him very quickly—unhappily married boss. He had been a youthful romantic idiot determined to play the big, protective hero… The memory of that long ago humiliation was enough to quash dead any impulse he might have felt to supply a shoulder for Matilda to cry on.

Self-contempt thinned his lips as he recalled the pathetic chivalry that had made him fantasise about rescuing her from her abusive husband and becoming a father to her children.

Just as well he hadn't. Fatherhood and him were not a good fit. He was too selfish. He was, in short, too like his own father. In Ezio's mind, it was better never to have a child than see that child grow up and feel no connection.

His father—a fully paid-up member of the '*it didn't do me any harm*' school of parenting—had replicated his own father's parenting style, which had not involved spontaneous displays of physical affection. *He* had started at the bottom, sweeping floors, and nobody had known that he was the *boss's* son. He'd wanted to instil the same standards in his own son.

So Ezio had arrived straight from university, just an anonymous office junior. It had never occurred to him to question his anonymity or suspect his identity had been revealed to senior management.

He considered that he had been lucky in his first boss, a woman who'd put on a brave face for the world but had allowed him to see the vulnerability beneath, had let him see her tears.

Hard to believe that he had ever been that stupid, that he had wanted to protect her. The principle that had put a married woman off-limits—back then he had had a lot of principles—had lasted barely a week.

He'd been in *love*. Before the self-contempt that always came with the memory could capture him, the sound of Matilda's sobs dragged him back to the present. Now she was crying softly, making him think of a wounded animal.

'S-sorry. I'll be fine in a minute.'

Ezio looked down at her bent head and swore. She looked so fragile, she looked so broken... Something shifted inside him and he swore again.

Then, without knowing what he was about to do, he heard himself growl out, 'Come here!'

Tilda lifted her head and looked from his face to his arms, extended towards her palms-up. With an inarticulate little cry, she took the two steps that landed her head on his chest. It didn't at that moment matter who he was, she needed the human contact.

The cry caused something painful he didn't recognise or enjoy to move in his chest as he looked down at the top of her glossy head, feeling her soft body shaking. Responding to some dormant instinct, his hands came up to her shoulders, even though he held himself rigid while her trembling body curved into his.

When she finally lifted her head, she looked embarrassed and backed away, her eyes anywhere but on him.

'I'm sorry...so sorry,' she sniffed. 'I never cry... well, hardly ever. I must look...'

She made him think of a shivering puppy. 'Sit down before you fall down,' he said, his voice roughened with an impatience he didn't attempt to disguise. What was the point? She could hardly think more badly of him than she evidently did.

It had never crossed his mind to wonder what any of the people he worked with thought of him, but knowing the thoughts that had been in his PA's head had touched an unexpected exposed nerve.

Tilda's legs folded as he urged her into a chair, not the designer one, but one of the soft leather swivels.

'Please don't be nice,' she begged, then remembered who she was talking to and laughed, stopping abruptly when she realised that she sounded borderline hysterical. 'I don't want to start crying again,' she explained.

'Neither do I,' he said.

His tone made her flush. 'Sorry, I'll be fine in a minute, it's just… You don't want to know this…'

He probably didn't. She was so close to disintegration that he could see no harm letting her talk if it calmed her down.

'It's therapeutic, so I have heard, and don't worry—I probably won't listen.'

The flash of dry humour dragged a small, choked laugh from her aching throat.

He did listen as she began to speak—not to him, really, more to herself, slowly at first, and then as if some sort of dam had broken inside her as it all spilled out.

The story had a lot of unnecessary details, and a vast amount of pointless hair-shirt self-loathing. But, picking out the salient points, the condensed version, even allowing for sisterly exaggeration, seemed to suggest that her brother was some sort of genius who had got in with the wrong crowd… 'Wrong crowd' got mentioned a lot.

'So everything that has happened to your brother is directly down to you?' This simplistic view stood out strongly throughout the jumbled narrative.

'Who else?' she snapped.

'Your brother is young but not a child. Don't you think he should take some responsibility for his own actions?'

'I knew you wouldn't understand. I have no idea why I told you any of this.' She shook her head. 'Oh, forget it!' she finished on a note of self-disgust as she got to her feet.

'So your brother is a genius…?'

'I don't know…probably. He's super smart, but I don't think labels help. But then, what do I know? I don't want to push him, I want him to have a normal life, a real childhood. He is desperate to blend in, but that's not easy when you pass your maths A-level at ten. I think that's when he stopped trying. I'm so afraid for him. I don't know what to do…'

Tilda put her head in her hands again. Well, stopping revealing her inner angst to a man who really didn't give a damn might be a start, but maybe that was the point—he didn't—and he wasn't going to feel sorry for her. How her independent nature hated it.

There had been a lot of that early on after the accident and her private nature had shied away from it. She had learnt to deflect pity, while practical help, which had been in thin supply, would have been much more useful.

Actually, Ezio's cold-eyed objectivity in some weird way acted as an antidote, or at least diluted her out-of-control emotions.

'Can I get you anything—a glass of water?'

Tilda shook her head. 'I'm fine.'

'Security has arrived.' The disembodied voice carried a chilly note of disapproval.

'What for? I don't need security! I need brandy.'

There was a nervous giggle on the other end of the line. 'How many glasses?'

He looked at his PA, the wispy curls that surrounded her heart-shaped face.

'Make that tea, some of the herbal stuff, for one.'

When the tea arrived, Tilda nursed the mug between her hands, looking at him warily over the rim. 'Aren't you having a cup?'

'I'll pass.'

'Look, I'm fine, I'm just…'

He sighed. 'About to fall down.'

This correct interpretation drew a glare from Tilda.

'Sit there a minute, I'm thinking…'

Her teeth clenched. 'I don't work for you any more. I don't have to do what you say.' She grimaced to hear herself sound so childish. Actually, he had never spoken to her so dismissively when they'd had a working relationship. If he had, she would have been looking for a new job a long time ago.

'You might have been right,' he mused slowly as he subjected her face to a narrow-eyed scrutiny.

'I usually am—you just don't notice.'

'I do, actually, you have a natural ability to think outside the box.'

'Is that a compliment?'

'It's a fact,' he responded without emphasis or warmth. 'You said that the best way to shut down Athena is to marry someone else.'

When it came to self-absorption, he really did run away with a string of gold medals.

'I might have said something along those lines but I wasn't being serious!'

'I am. I think it could work.'

An image of Ezio married, his arm around a glowing bride, flashed into her head. 'Well, that's great—problem solved.' Only a man as cynical and without any moral compass would have taken her angry words seriously.

She put down her mug on the top of his pristine desk. She had no idea if he was winding her up or if he was serious, and she told herself she didn't care.

'I'll look out for the marriage announcement,' she said, making her voice flat and disinterested.

'Sit down, will you, Matilda?'

'My name is *Tilda*!'

He accepted the correction with an expressive shrug of disinterest. 'Six months… *Tilda*?' His lips quirked as he rolled the word around his tongue. 'What do you say?'

'That I pity the woman you marry unless she has as little moral compass as you.'

His lip curled. 'I think you have enough *moral compass* for us both.'

He made it sound like a bad thing.

'But I no longer work for you and now, if you'd excuse me, I'll get my things and leave you to—' She stopped as he held up a hand, asking her to wait. She sighed. 'Look, I recognise this is not convenient for you, but I have to put my brother first. I have to move him away from—'

'The bad influences, I know... Would Greece be far enough, you think?'

Confusion replaced her annoyance. 'Greece!' She had never been to the Athens office but she had seen the views from the board room during online meetings; they were stunning. 'Is Agnes leaving too?' Tilda had met the elegant, grey-haired half-Greek woman who held her own role in the Athens office.

Even if there was a vacancy there was no way she could move to Athens...could she?

'No, Agnes is not leaving, and I'm not offering you a job. More a *role*... You could think of it as a temporary contract...six months?'

'Is it a promotion?' She was in no position to dismiss it out of hand. Something with more flexibility would give her time to look for something more appropriate. But Greece? No, that was *too* crazy... too far away. Though maybe far away was good?

'That kind of depends on your viewpoint.'

She muted the dialogue in her head and decided there was no harm hearing him out. 'It's real?' Her history of being around him told her it was not likely to be an invention, but she had to check. 'I'm not a charity case.'

He sighed. 'I'm suggesting that we spend the next six months as husband and wife, so basically six months in Greece, long enough to make people think we gave it a try and you found me impossible to live with.'

Shock collided with disbelief in her spinning head. Her brain went into shock and closed down.

'Obviously there is a time factor involved. This has to happen... I'll look into how quickly this *can* happen. It probably won't be the UK. I don't think you are able to book a slot Vegas-style here.'

'I suppose you know that you make it sound as though you're proposing to me?' She felt stupid even saying it.

'I'm proposing a way in which you can remove your brother from people and an environment that have become dangerous for him, while killing Athena's rumours that are stalling the Rutherford deal...' He flashed a look at her pale, still face. 'So, win-win. Are you all right?'

'I think I'm the one that should be asking you that,' she responded hoarsely. 'Is there *nothing* you wouldn't do to win?'

His devil-on-steroids white grin flashed. 'I don't like losing,' he admitted. 'That's no secret. But I think the relevant question is, is this something *you* would be prepared to do for your brother?'

Having succeeded in making her rejection of the plan prove she was selfish, he tilted his head to one side, his stare making her feel uneasy. He was good, he was very good, but she had seen him use this tactic before—actually, that didn't help.

Ezio felt his impatience rise as she didn't react, then another reason for her reticence occurred to him. 'Is there someone?' Contemplating the possibility that his PA had a personal life, a sex life, brought a wrinkle to his brow. There was no reason she shouldn't, that someone should not be enjoying the lush, sensual promise of her mouth. 'I got the idea that if he were twenty years younger Saul might be a rival.'

'Are you suggesting that I flirted with…?' She gave a gasp of outrage. 'If anyone is being unprofessional here, it's you, not me!'

He opened his mouth to deny this claim and then realised that she was right…he sounded like a jealous lover. 'All right, I concede, you're probably not his type.'

'Or yours,' she added. 'And, actually, you've hit on the obvious flaw, beyond the fact it is insane, obviously.'

His dark brows climbed towards his ebony hairline. 'I have?'

'We both know that a billionaire of any age does not marry a woman like me.'

'You don't think you're attractive enough?' As he was sure it took her longer to disguise the fact she was attractive than it would have done to moderately enhance her good looks, it seemed a perverse attitude to take.

Detecting his slight sneer and misreading it, her jaw tightened. 'My self-confidence is quite robust, thank you,' she told him crisply. 'It so happens my self-worth is not based on the way I look—though, actually, I scrub up pretty well.'

The huffy addition made his lips twitch.

'I am quite sure you do.'

'But my problem is, I don't want to devote twenty per cent of my life to the pursuit of polished perfection, the sort of gloss that can't be achieved without good lighting and a master class in make-up. I wouldn't do that for any man.'

'You think that's what I want in a woman?'

'I think that's what you and most obscenely wealthy men *expect* in a woman,' she countered.

'So basically I'm shallow.'

'You're obscenely rich.'

It was pretty obvious she had based this harsh judgement of the '*obscenely* rich' on him. It came as a shock to know how the woman he had worked with for four years had been silently judging him. The question was, did he deserve it?

Ezio brushed away the question. The only reason to find out would be if he wanted to change—and he didn't.

'I wasn't talking about you…'

She stopped digging. They both knew she was, and why should she worry? It wasn't as if Ezio was going to cry into his pillow because she wasn't giving him a five-star review.

'Shall we just say joke over…? It's crazy…?' The upward lilt on the last syllable that turned her statement into a question made him give a smug grin.

'Audacious and actually, when you think about it, totally logical. I know you like logic.' He knew she considered herself the voice of reason, and there had been occasions when she had been.

'I'm simply not a risk taker.'

'You're capable, smart and have no great opinion of…well, me, but I also believe you are pragmatic. This might not be a palatable solution to you but it is a solution,' he pointed out, appreciating the novelty value of having to sell a prospect that any number of women would have spent a lot of time and energy trying to bring about.

'You are proposing this seriously…it's not a joke?'

'You're not normally five steps behind.'

'No, just two.'

Her dry rejoinder drew a slow grin before it faded quickly as he continued, all brisk and business-like. 'Obviously we can come to some sort of severance agreement upfront which will give you and your brother financial security.'

'But I can't just transplant us. There are schools and…'

He smiled to himself. He knew that schools would earn him points. 'Actually, I know of a school within traveling distance of the villa. It has an international reputation and an...*eclectic* approach to education. It has a child-first policy, the ethos is—'

'You seem to know a lot about this place.' Comprehension dawned on her face. 'You went there?'

'Let's just say I was not thriving in the school my father and his father before him went to.' It was one of the rare occasions when his mother had defied her husband and insisted that there was a tradition in her family too, one that said children should not be unhappy. 'I spent my last three years in school there.'

'And that is a recommendation...? Sorry,' she said, instantly remorseful. 'That was below the belt.'

His smile was rueful. 'Do not worry, I can take it. I was simply pointing out that there is no need to see problems where there are none.'

'This place sounds expensive.'

'It is, but that will not be a problem for you now or in the future. In fact, money would never be an issue for you again. Or your brother,' he emphasised, watching her face, well aware that her devotion to her sibling was the edge he needed, and having no qualms about exploiting this weakness.

'Villa, you said. Villa...?' Am I *really* considering this?

'My home—'

'*One* of them,' Tilda interrupted, going through

a mental inventory of his penthouse apartments in several cities, the estate in Surrey that she had seen photos of in a glossy magazine, and where she knew for a fact that he had never spent a night. She suspected he'd never even seen it.

It was an investment; he had no emotional attachment to it. He had no emotional attachment to anything. Did he even know what a home was? A home in her mind was what she shared with Sam— the place her parents had bought when they'd first married. It held memories and it was Sam's security.

'It has privacy, a view and is a short helicopter flight from the Athens office.'

'I thought you had a house in Athens… Never mind; I'm sure your villa is delightful, but I live here.'

'I thought you were planning to move to Cornwall.'

Her eyes slid from his. She was not quite ready to concede defeat yet. 'I haven't decided what I'm going to do.'

'I understand your reluctance—you don't want to drag Sam away from all his delightful friends.'

She flinched as if he had struck her, and there it was—he knew he had closed the deal.

He gave a slow smile of satisfaction. 'It should be champagne, really,' he observed, looking at the half-empty mug.

She ignored the mug and him. 'I need to get back to Sam. I said—'

'Fine. It will be a good opportunity for me to meet Sam and we can get into the details on the way back.'

She looked at him blankly. 'Meet Sam? No, you can't, you have a meeting at… Oh, and you're picking up Ellie Watts for early dinner before the premiere of her film.'

'I think I might cancel that, don't you?' he said softly.

'You can't! She… Well, she's *her*, and they say that she's the odds-on favourite for best actress.' And according to rumour the latest notch on his bedpost, or was *he* the latest notch on *hers*?

'And I just got engaged. Think of the optics when someone works out the dates.'

'But no one knows, and we're not *really* engaged. It takes a long time to get a licence and things sorted. I thought that…'

Actually, she had not thought at all, that much was becoming obvious. 'I haven't said yes.' But she hadn't said no either, and his expression said he knew she wasn't going to.

'You wish me to get down on one knee?'

She cast a withering look at his handsome, mocking face.

'It's happening too quickly,' she complained.

CHAPTER THREE

'IF SAM HATES YOU, it's off!'

He looked amused and a little contemptuous. 'You allow a *child* to dictate how you live your life?'

Explaining the concept involved to someone who had never considered anyone in his life but himself seemed a waste of time and energy to Tilda, so instead she closed the conversation down. 'Of course not!'

'My mistake,' he drawled sarcastically.

'And for God's sake, don't call him a child.'

'What do you take me for? I was fourteen once, you know, in the dim and distant past.'

She grunted. She found it impossible to imagine Ezio suffering the traumas of a normal teen.

'My phone, where did I…?' Irritated by the greasy smear on her glasses, she pulled them off and began polishing them vigorously on a tissue. She rubbed the bridge of her pert nose before she put them back on.

Ezio seemed to freeze for a moment, then blinked. 'You have beautiful eyes.'

The personal comment came from nowhere. Tilda, conscious of a shivery sensation that spread outwards from a centre low in her pelvis, brought her lashes down behind the lenses as a further layer of protection.

'Have you thought of contact lenses?'

The tension she had probably imagined dissolved as she laughed. 'Oh, when I do, you will be the very *first* person I will consult on the decision.' Behind her smile of mocking and fake sincerity, she was aware that her show of empowerment might have carried a bit more punch if she'd actually *needed* the glasses.

Rowena was hovering when they walked out of the office.

'We're going out.'

Rowena nodded and glanced at the box of Tilda's belongings on the desk.

'Shall I...?' she asked, her nervous glance flickering from one to the other.

'Leave it there,' Ezio responded at his most enigmatically distant as he started punching numbers into his phone.

Turning round as they approached the lift, Tilda gave a thumbs up to the younger girl and promptly backed into Ezio.

'Sorry, I'm...' He arched a brow and she stepped inside, taking a deep breath. She knew from experience that Ezio and enclosed spaces was not a combination that made for comfortable—*more crawl out of your skin.*

Ezio had very long legs, and she did not, but it didn't occur to him to make any allowances for the difference in their inside leg measurements, and by the time they reached the underground parking area she was breathless and very glad she was wearing trainers.

'Did you see Rowena's face?' she asked fretfully as she responded to his imperious nod and fastened the belt of the passenger seat in the limited-edition designer car he drove. It was not exactly inconspicuous but it was comfortable.

'Rowena's face?'

'No, you wouldn't.' His radar was very specific and Rowena had not been on it. Whoever he'd been texting, he had been on his phone since they had left the office.

If they were together in the real sense of the word she would have dumped him before they reached the underground parking area.

'I was setting things in motion. It's looking like New York state is our best option…unless you fancy a Vegas wedding? I've got a really good wedding planner on it, and she'll sort the options, but New York is sounding good to me. I have a few things that I could do with checking on at the office there.'

'I think that's what you call hitting the ground running but, before you go the extra mile, let me be clear—*if* we do this, it won't be in New York while you multi-task,' she responded, matching his cool with some of her own.

The car purred into almost silent life. 'Why not? It's a twenty-eight-day wait in the UK.'

'It's not the place, it's the entire concept.'

'Never mind. The next time you can do it right— white lace and orange blossom and a house in a district with the best schools—but just remember to keep the number of a very good divorce lawyer for when reality kicks in.'

'You are such a cynic!' His mockery was making her teeth ache.

'Realist,' he countered, sketching a grim smile as he pulled into the stream of traffic.

'I feel sorry for you,' she countered, almost meaning it. 'It's in this country or nowhere, and this time frame is all too...' Her head lifted. 'I need time to think.'

'You could think about it for weeks, months, but it wouldn't change the essentials. This will work for us both. Now, where am I going?'

She refused to be diverted; she'd given too much ground already. 'The UK.'

He glanced at her profile and sighed. 'I'll invite Saul to the wedding. That should get around the problem of the unnecessary delay.'

His immediate response made it clear to Tilda that he had always had Plan B in place. 'Oh no, I don't want anyone there!'

'Don't worry, he'll refuse. I'll make sure the date

coincides with his granddaughter's wedding. The point is, he'll know we are getting married.'

'You are so Machiavellian!'

'Thank you. So, which way?'

'Nice house.' It was a solid-looking Edwardian property in a quiet tree-lined road of other similar properties in North London. He probably didn't mean it but Mrs Lowther, who got flustered and giggly when she was introduced to the visitor, didn't know that. Once in the door, he charmed the old lady into her coat and escorted her home.

It was quite a master class in charm.

Sam was less impressed. 'What did you fetch *him* home for?'

'He fetched me home, actually.'

'I thought your boss was a selfish bastard who…'

She flashed him a warning look as the tingle between her shoulder blades alerted her to Ezio's presence.

'I've heard a lot about you, Sam.' Ezio had to make his remark to the narrow, hostile back of the teen he was meant to be impressing. Tilda doubted that Ezio could recall the last time in his life he'd tried to impress someone.

'I've heard more about you, I bet. Ezio… Ezio… Ezio…' Sam mocked, ignoring his sister's horrified expression as he added, 'She's always talking about Ezio this, Ezio that.'

'I am not, Sam!' Tilda said, shaking her head as

Ezio's dark eyes skimmed her flushed face. 'That's not true.'

Or was it? The disturbing possibility brought a frown to her smooth brow.

'I called my goldfish Ezio when I was a kid.'

And now you're so old. 'I'm flattered. Good goldfish?'

'Dead goldfish,' Sam came back with a straight face.

The teen watched suspiciously as Ezio threw his head back and laughed. 'I hear you are smart, Sam.'

'Yeah, a lot of people are intimidated. Tilda is quite bright too, you know—well, above average.'

From where she had dropped into a chair Tilda, gave a laugh. 'Why, thank you!' she drawled sarcastically.

'But she's a bit of an innocent, people take advantage.' Sam shot Ezio a glare before adding in a guilty aside, 'Including me.'

Ezio took the warning from the skinny little fourteen-year-old with an appreciative nod.

'Fancy a game?' Sam said casually, nodding towards the screen he'd been crouched over.

Tilda's eyes flew wide as she shook her head emphatically. 'Sam, Ezio *doesn't*.'

'Ezio does,' her ex-boss and future husband contradicted, taking off his jacket before looping it across the back of one of the dining chairs, dragging it into position next to Sam's chair and straddling it.

Her last chance had been Sam hating him, but

against all the odds Sam *wasn't* hating him. After he beat Ezio at the computer game, they bonded some more over a game of chess, after which winner Sam declared it a *close* game…a massive compliment, coming from her brother.

'You're too good for me,' Ezio said, polishing his rusty humility.

'You must be hungry, Sam, and Ezio has to be… Somewhere to go…?' She sent Ezio a nod of encouragement. 'Didn't you say that you had to…?'

'I cancelled remember? And you are definitely too tired to cook,' he continued his lips twitching at the killer look she had slung him. 'How about take away?' The ease with which he had adopted a pattern of easy familiarity made her grit her teeth.

She resented that he was very much setting the pace, taking control, but her hands were tied.

After some debate, pizza was decided on, and her choice of pineapple on top was treated with universal contempt.

My God, she thought, listening as her brother and her ex-boss and soon-to-be husband bonded over their shared loathing of pineapple on pizza and love of chess. If this day could have got any more surreal, she didn't know how.

She knew it was all an act on Ezio's part, but she had to admit, the man he was pretending to be ticked a lot of boxes. If that man had existed, she would have been in love in seconds. The acknowledgment created a sense of unease that she couldn't shake.

It was still there when, midway through the pizza, Ezio dropped the bombshell without any warning or consultation.

'I asked your sister to marry me and she said yes, Sam, but you have the casting vote. We'd be moving to Greece, which would be a big thing for you, so what do you think?'

'What? You're getting married? And... Greece?' Sam looked at his sister for confirmation. 'For real?'

She nodded, hiding her annoyance that Ezio had made a unilateral decision to move the situation to the next level. If and when Sam was told, it should have been her doing the telling.

'Would that mean I wouldn't have to go back to school here?'

She nodded again. 'It would mean a lot of changes,' she admitted.

Sam's grunt in response could have meant anything but there was no misinterpreting the sag of relief in his narrow shoulders, a measure of just how much he was dreading going back to school.

Tilda's eyes misted. She was making the right choice.

'We have schools in Greece, some good ones. I could email you links...?'

'I'd need to learn the language?' The prospect of the challenge brought a glitter to the teen's eyes, which faded as he added, 'It doesn't really matter. I'll still be a weird loser there. The freak!'

Lost for words to comfort him, it broke Tilda's heart to hear him voice fears she shared.

'I got called weird and worse a few times at school.'

Brother and sister both turned in unison to stare at him, varying degrees of disbelief in their faces.

'You!' It was Sam who expressed the doubts written on both Raven faces.

'Uh-huh. There is a good ending to this story, though. You know what those boys who called me weirdo do when they see me now?'

Sam shook his head.

'They smile politely and call me *sir…* They work for me.'

Sam looked thoughtful for a moment, then his thin face broke into a smile. 'That is cool.'

'It is actually *extremely* cool,' Ezio agreed. 'It's also cool being the smartest person in the room, though I should warn you, you probably wouldn't always be in the Athens academy. Right, then, I'll email you and Tilda the school stuff, Sam.' He turned and delivered one of his best megawatt smiles to Tilda as he got to his feet.

She suddenly felt a little more understanding of the women at whom he smiled and meant it—it was not hard to imagine that smile becoming a recreational drug of choice!

'Like to walk me to the door?' He held out a hand to her.

Aware that Sam was watching, after a second she

stretched her hand out and allowed it to be enfolded inside the cool of his long, brown fingers. The moment they were out of the room, she pulled it free. The tingling sensation didn't stop even when she rubbed her hand hard against her thigh, only stopping to open the door for him.

'That was kind of you.' She nodded her head towards the sitting room door and added huskily, 'With Sam.'

He gave a dismissive shrug. 'Not kind. It will help if he doesn't resent me and, yes, it was true... I know you're dying to ask.' The corners of his mouth lifted, matching the smile glinting in his eyes. 'The only slight deceit was not telling him that I was not so good at turning the other cheek...' One dark brow lifted to a sardonic angle. 'Humiliate a bully and word gets around and it takes the target off your back.'

'Or it puts a target on your back for anyone who wants to prove they're tough.'

'That is not my experience, so relax; I don't think Sam is the physical type.'

But you are, she thought. As her eyes drifted down his hard, lean body, she swallowed hard and veiled her shocked eyes, feeling the soft flutter that had resided low in her belly all evening get stronger.

Less butterfly and more trapped bird.

'I sincerely hope he isn't.'

'A defensive martial art might make him feel

more confident.' He saw her expression and lifted his palms towards her. 'Just a thought.'

'One I'd be grateful if you kept to yourself. Violence,' she said primly, 'Is no answer to anything, and the idea of my brother's hands being a lethal weapon would not make me sleep well.'

As she spoke, her eyes got tugged towards Ezio's hands, one of which was braced on the doorframe, long, elegant fingers that probably knew their way around a woman's body.

The rogue thought sent a rush of shamed heat through her body. Where had that come from? She channelled her ashamed confusion, resurrecting her earlier annoyance.

'And, for the record, telling Sam about us—the us we are pretending exists—was *my* job, not *yours*. You don't know Sam and—'

'And you'd like to keep it that way…fair enough,' he agreed, his expression not matching his careless shrug.

'That wasn't what I was saying,' she said, annoyed he was twisting what she *was* saying. It would have been helpful if she'd known what she was saying!

'I accept I'm uniquely ill-equipped to parent, but I actually like Sam.'

She could see the surprise she could hear in his voice reflected for a moment in his dark eyes.

'I *love* Sam, and he'll always come first for me.'

'And where does that leave you when you're no

longer first for Sam? You might not think so now, but that time will come.'

'You think I don't know that?' Her amusement was genuine and her throaty laughter was extremely attractive, he realised. 'Sam is a teenage boy. I already come second to any number of things. I'm not clingy; I want him to be happy, to leave home… knowing he can always come back. You must remember when your parents stopped being the most important things in your life? But you remain the most important thing in theirs.'

She watched as an expression she couldn't put a name to drifted into his eyes but it was gone so quickly that she thought she had imagined it.

'How old were you when yours died?'

'Almost twenty.'

'That must have been…' He stopped. Saying '*hard*' seemed hopelessly inadequate.

'It's hard when you realise there isn't anyone you're the most important thing in the world for any more. I swore Sam wouldn't feel like that.'

A silence followed her words.

Tilda had never imagined sharing those innermost private thoughts with anyone before and, if she had, the last person in the world she could have imagined opening up to was Ezio.

'Well, goodnight,' she blurted when the silence got too uncomfortable to bear. 'Oh, and shall I come in the normal time tomorrow, or do you need me early for the meeting with—?'

'No, don't come in. You're not my PA now, you're my bride-to-be.'

She looked surprised. 'But…we don't have to tell anyone yet.'

'I have no intention of telling anyone except Saul.'

'Not your family?'

'My mother would ask too many awkward questions and want to meet you.' His expressive lips thinned in distaste as he observed, 'My father would probably make a pass at you.'

Before she could decide if he was being serious, without any warning he casually leaned in. Tilda felt corralled by his sheer physicality and panic nipped at her as she felt the warmth of his breath stir the fine hairs along her hairline. She stiffened and fought against the slow, dreamy feeling that was invading her body, the weird floating sensation accompanying the heavy thud of her heart.

'There, got it.' He straightened up, opened his hand and a moth fluttered into the night air. 'It got tangled in your hair.'

'Oh, right, yes. I…'

'Do you need the tint in your specs?' he asked.

Tilda pressed a finger to the dark plastic that rested on the bridge of her nose, dodging his stare. 'It's not a matter of *need*. I *like* them this way,' she lied. 'So sorry you don't like glasses.'

He looked surprised. 'Did I say that?'

'No, but…'

A flicker of a smile played across the sensual line of his lips. 'I think there is something quite sexy about glasses…depending on who is wearing them, obviously.'

'Well, I know I'm not,' she blurted.

'What, sexy…?'

'No, I… I'm not interested in what you think is sexy.' She already knew it involved endless legs and curves.

The erotic images that flickered through Ezio's head effectively nailed him to the spot for several humiliating, painful heart beats, so until his control reasserted itself he cloaked his eyes with half-lowered lids.

Ezio had spent years enjoying sex without commitment and, now this situation was about to be reversed, commitment without sex did not sound nearly so pleasurable to him at that moment.

They said you could get used to anything.

'I'm light-sensitive,' she said. 'I don't know how it works, but these—' she tapped the frame '—don't affect my colour perception. It's more, I can see you but you can't see me.'

'Convenient.'

Looking panicked, she gave a little shrug as their glances locked. The air was suddenly filled with a painful, nerve-scraping tension.

'Sorry!' she blurted out, breaking it.

He lifted a dark brow. 'Sorry for…?'

'Oh, well, sorry you missed out on your film premiere. Speaking of which, I know six months is a long time for you to...' She broke off, blushing wildly as she dodged his eyes. 'But I'm realistic. I'm fine with...you know... But because of Sam can you please be discreet if you understand what I'm saying?'

'Actually not saying.' She was skirting around the subject like some sort of Victorian virgin. But he understood all right and he had no idea why it made him so angry. 'Shall I save you the bother? You're giving me permission to screw around.'

Her head jerked back at the crudity and she glanced back anxiously towards the closed sitting room door. 'I know you don't need my permission,' she admitted. 'And I'm not trying to, I'm just asking you... Look, Sam seems to like you, and I don't want him thinking of women, relationships, as... I want him to respect women.'

'I didn't ask to be a role model,' Ezio rebutted, his sardonic smile forced as he thought of the role model in life—his father. His father who had never needed permission to screw around, or seen any need not to flaunt his numerous affairs.

'No,' she conceded. 'But you asked me to marry you and Sam and I...we are a package deal,' she reminded him with stressed, forced calm. 'I'm not asking you to take a vow of celibacy, not with your... er...appetites.' He could see her cheeks flaming again and she stopped and closed her eyes, clearly wishing that she had not started this conversation.

'Where are you going?' she called after him as he abruptly walked through the door.

He turned back and produced a fixed feral smile. 'Well, I thought I might live down to your opinion of me and slake my animal urges with a woman I don't respect while I still don't have to ask for permission.'

The retort brought an angry glitter to her eyes. 'She has my sympathy,' she snapped as she slammed the door.

Tilda took a few sense-cooling moments before she returned to her brother and the million questions he felt the need to ask. The one she found most difficult to answer being the gruffly delivered, *'I can see why you want to marry him, but why so quickly? Shouldn't you live together or something first? If this goes wrong you could get hurt, Tilda.'*

Tilda had done her best to counter his concerns, pointing out that they might not have been dating very long—luckily Sam didn't ask *how* long—but they were not exactly strangers.

She was actually very touched by the brotherly concern which brought into focus the elephant in the room that Ezio seemed determined to ignore— nobody on the planet would believe that the most gorgeous man on earth would choose her over the glorious Athena Baros, she of the endless legs and much-copied pout.

This 'married to the PA' scheme, it simply wasn't *believable*. Tilda couldn't understand for the life of her why *she* was the only one who could see that.

It wasn't about self-confidence; Tilda wasn't intimidated by the Athena Baroses of this world. She didn't feel envious...except *possibly* when it came to leg length.

She had a lot to offer a relationship when she found the right man, who would hopefully be looking for those qualities. The point was the things she had to offer were not the things that Ezio was looking for outside the work environment.

He was out there looking for that right now—*superficially sexy*. It was a deeply depressing thought.

CHAPTER FOUR

TILDA KNEW BECAUSE she kept his diary, or had, that Ezio had a crammed, wall-to-wall schedule in the month running up to the wedding, so it wasn't very surprising that she saw him only twice. On both occasions he had spent the majority of the visits focusing on Sam, playing chess, discovering a shared interest in philosophy and generally making her feel intellectually inadequate.

But her brother was happy so she was prepared to forgive Ezio a lot... Not that he was ignoring her, *exactly*, but he did seem to be keeping her at a distance. Maybe it was a subliminal message and he was just signalling the way he meant things to go on.

Oh, God, was she over-thinking this? He was just treating her the way he always had. Actually, no, he wasn't; she had never felt excluded before.

The time would have gone quicker if she had just gone back to the office and resumed her previous role until the wedding, but Ezio had been adamant that it wouldn't be appropriate for her to continue working for him under the circumstances. And she had to admit she couldn't quite imagine how that would have worked either.

So Tilda found herself in a bizarre situation of being secretly engaged to a man she had been used to seeing most working days but now barely saw at all.

As for any influence she might once have had, now she had none.

She didn't miss Ezio's presence in her life, *obviously*, but she was conscious of a massive gap that had opened up—which was not the same thing at all. While she had been cast into the wilderness, he was probably fitting in a lot of pre-marital sex *to slake his animal urges* before he got lumbered with her.

If this was what the *now* was like, what were the next six months going to be like…and after? Quickly tiring of moping around aimlessly, she made herself think about the future. She needed a plan. Sure, when the marriage ended she would not be poor, but there was no way she was going sit around doing nothing.

There were things that she'd always thought she would like to do if she had either the time or the money and now she was about to have both.

In that awful time after their parents had died, and Tilda had been left trying to comfort her grieving brother and be a parent, there had not been a lot of time to think about what *she* needed and not a lot of accessible help out there.

There had been dark moments, lonely moments, but she knew there were people who had it a lot worse than she did. They had the house, the memories and the financial cushion of a small insurance pot that had supplemented her first pay cheques. Not everyone was so lucky.

A chance encounter at a bus stop as she'd helped a girl load her mum and the older woman's wheelchair onto the bus had brought home how much worse her situation could have been. The girl, barely older than Sam, had been acting as her disabled mum's main carer and going to school.

She remembered thinking how good it would be to be in a position to help all those people like that girl, and for that matter people in the situation she had been in—people in situations where they were isolated and alone. At the most basic, provide someone to talk to, or point them in the right direction to access to available funding, a support network.

She remembered thinking that if she had the money and the time she could have made it happen.

Well, now she had both.

As she put down the phone after hanging up on Saul Rutherford, she felt a glow of achievement. She'd taken her first step towards the future she had envisaged.

She hadn't planned it. She had rung him to thank him in person for the massive bouquet he'd sent her to congratulate her on her future wedding. But it was Saul who had turned the quick courtesy call into something else when he had proceeded to ask her straight out, with zero subtlety, if she minded that Ezio was cheating on her. Tilda had not been thrown. She had not worked with Ezio for four years for nothing; she could think on her feet.

She had assured him calmly that the stories circulating were malicious and untrue. Crossing her fingers, she'd felt only the tiniest flicker of guilt when she'd said she trusted Ezio with her life. She must have sounded sincere because he had apologised.

Well, it wasn't a total lie. If she were to be stuck in a burning building, or facing down a gang of knife-wielding, drug-crazed thugs, she wouldn't doubt Ezio's ability to rescue her...or that he would.

He was one of those men, the heroes of this world, who best functioned, and in fact thrived in fact in, high-stress scenarios... They were rumoured to struggle with life in the real boring, mundane world, though Ezio seemed to have that under control too.

Trusting him with her life—yes. Trusting him with her heart was another matter. Luckily, hearts had not been mentioned in any of the copious documents she had read before she'd signed away the next six months of her life.

She had told an apologetic Saul she was not the least offended and then had asked him for his advice. He'd been generous with it, and equally generous when he'd offered not just useful contacts he'd made when setting up his own charity, but a very generous donation.

The upcoming marriage was keeping the lawyers busy. She had stopped envying them their workload.

She was no longer adrift, she had a purpose and she had a future waiting for her when her six-month marriage secondment, as she liked to think of it, was over.

So, while she was immersing herself in her new venture, she was quietly crossing off the twenty-eight days on her calendar before the day ringed in red arrived, pretending she was totally cool with it.

Even though anything important to do with the wedding had been taken out of her hands, there were a lot of incidentals, and then there were the practicalities. If Sam settled and was happy at the Greek school, she planned to take somewhere small in Athens and become fully involved in the charity.

It might be an idea to learn the language, though harder for her than Sam. It was never an ego-enhancing idea to compare herself with her brilliant brother, who made things look easy.

The prospect of not going back to the local school meant Sam was looking happier than she'd seen him in an age. Considering she had worried about selling the idea to him, it was ironic that if she'd backed out he'd never forgive her—though that wasn't fair, as he had told her that if she changed her mind he'd be fine with it.

But his reaction when she said she wasn't changing her mind spoke volumes. She wasn't backing out and if she did there was nowhere much to go back to. She was committed, and the physical evidence of her commitment was sitting on her finger.

She held her hand up to the light. The engagement ring had been couriered over to her that very morning, a massive square emerald surrounded by black diamonds. It fitted perfectly.

She was the one who didn't fit!

'It's here!' Sam yelled, watching out for the limo that was taking them to the registry office. 'You should see the curtains twitching. Not really,' he added as Tilda walked up behind him, looking worried.

At the front door they both paused, Sam looking smart and scrubbed in his new suit and suddenly looking almost as nervous as she felt.

'You look very pretty,' he said awkwardly.

Smiling at the brotherly compliment, she glanced down, smoothing the fabric of her recycled dress. It had still had the tags on and hadn't even made it to the charity shop's racks when she'd caught sight of the hand-sewn label. She'd bought it on the spot, drawn not just by the designer credentials but the simple empire line lifted by the hand embroidery around the neckline. Apart from needing a couple of inches taken off the length, it had fitted perfectly. She remembered thinking as she'd twirled in front of the mirror that all she needed now was somewhere to wear it.

Her sensitive tummy flipped. Now she did have somewhere to wear her recycled bargain: her own wedding.

'Thank you, so do you.'

They had reached the car when Tilda stopped and gave a sudden decisive nod. 'Wait a minute.'

'Don't ask me, mate,' Sam said at the question on the driver's face as his sister dashed off.

A few moments later, Tilda returned. 'I had to tell Mrs Lowther and say goodbye,' she said as she slid into the limo. 'She's been so good to us. She said I look like Mum,' she added as Sam sat back, having fastened his seat belt.

'You don't.'

'I know that, but it was so sweet of her.'

He looked alarmed. 'You're not going to cry, are you?'

'God, no!'

'I wish Mum was here, and Dad…you know?'

Tilda squeezed his hand. She did know. 'Me too, every day,' she said softly. 'If they were, I wouldn't be here at all,' she began with wistful regret before making contact with her brother's questioning gaze. She made a swift recovery. 'Mum would have insisted on a full church white wedding with hundreds of guests and I'd be floating down the aisle in miles of tulle.'

'Yeah, I guess so. I don't really remember her as well as you do.' Sam turned his head to gaze out of the window but not before Tilda had seen the moisture in his eyes. 'I've never seen the streets this empty. You're going to be married before the rest of the world is awake.'

'Mum and Dad would have been proud of you, Sam,' she said softly.

'I know I don't say it, but I am grateful for all the stuff you have done for me. I think this is us,' he added before Tilda could respond.

'Isn't it fashionable for the bride to be late?'

'You sound jittery. Perhaps I should get him to drive us around the block one more time.'

'Too late,' she murmured as the driver opened the door for her. 'Thanks,' she said as she squared her shoulders, took a deep breath and slid out, refusing to let panic take charge.

Bending down to adjust the heel strap on her suede sling-back that didn't need adjusting, her attempt to slow her heart beat failed when on the periphery of her vision she saw a tall figure crossing the road.

From the other side of the limo, she heard Sam yell out a greeting.

Tilda smothered the panic and pasted on a smile before using her posy as a shield as she turned to face him. The knot in her stomach tightened as she took in the details of his achingly perfect appearance.

Ezio was wearing a superbly cut formal dress suit, looking the epitome of style—not that anyone would be talking fashion; they'd be talking about the gorgeous, handsome man they were picturing minus the clothes.

Or is that just me?

He always carried himself with the careless confidence and grace of a natural athlete. The aura of command he projected sent a tingle through her body before he even got close enough to speak.

'You got the flowers.' Ezio took in the dress, noting it was none of the designer ones he'd had sent over, but it was the epitome of understated feminine elegance and it fitted her slim figure perfectly. Cut to a couple of inches above the knee, it showcased her stupendously shapely legs and narrow ankles in a way that sent a stream of searing heat down his body.

She'd looked composed but that illusion was ruined the moment he got close enough to see her eyes behind the new cat's eye frames she was wearing. Startlingly green and wary, they made him think of a wild thing likely to bolt if startled.

'Thank you, they are beautiful, and smell gorgeous.' She lifted the bouquet to her nose.

His eyes moved upwards with the action but only as far as the pale skin above the square necked bodice that fitted snugly over her small, high breasts, revealing the finest suggestion of a cleavage and the delicate angularity of her collar bones.

Aware that he had been staring for…well, actually he had no idea how long…he cleared his throat. 'Pretty necklace.' It matched the earrings, the small studs with a pearl inset he had noticed she wore every day.

'Thanks, it was my mother's. And the ring, it's

very…' She held her hand at an angle to expose the green glitter on her ring finger. 'It really…'

'Not too much,' he inserted, predicting her next words exactly.

'It is very beautiful. I'll keep it safe for you,' she promised.

'Keep it safe?'

'It was a family heirloom…the setting looks antique.'

'It is antique but not an heirloom. But I thought it would match your eyes…'

As their glances connected, Tilda experienced a spike of panicky excitement which she fought to subdue. There was no subtext; there was nothing to read into his voice, baring the obvious fact he could have made an ingredient label on a soup can sound sexy.

'Sam and I inherited Mum's eyes, but she was a redhead,' Tilda murmured as her gaze moved beyond him as though she had discovered some fascinating architectural details in the still-closed art deco building. 'Are we early?' she said, frowning as she heard the over-bright, perky note in her voice.

'Not much. They agreed to open early for us, so we will not be seeing our photos posted online,' he observed with a degree of grim satisfaction. 'It should be a quick in and out.'

'Quick in and out…?' She wasn't looking for romance, but it was hard not to supress a tiny grimace.

She saw his glance sharpen and added quickly,

'Oh, that's good. Perfect.' Escaping his stare, she turned her gaze to the trio of men standing on the steps of the registry office across the road. 'Are they with us?'

Ezio, who had pulled his phone from his pocket and was glaring at it, was still frowning when he looked at her.

'They are our witnesses.' He offered the explanation readily enough but she could see his mind was elsewhere.

She assumed he was talking about two of the three men waiting on the steps of the building, the two in suits. It was the third she was curious about. It was hard to see how he fitted in. In faded torn denims and a tee shirt, with shaggy white-blond hair, it was easy to imagine him carrying a surf board, but actually he was carrying a canvas bag slung over his shoulder, so there remained a bit of a question mark over his role.

She waited until Ezio put his phone away and moved towards her.

'Legal department?' she asked, nodding without looking to the two suits.

'Thought I'd keep it in-house.'

'A need-to-know basis,' she mocked gently, wondering if she had broken his rules by telling Mrs Lowther earlier. 'Lawyers always look like lawyers,' she added, making an unashamedly untrue generalisation as she stared curiously at the third man.

'Our official photographer.' As if he'd heard, the

guy pulled a camera out of the bulging bag and began fiddling with dials in what seemed like an expert way.

'Come say hello.'

Very conscious of the hand on the middle of her back as they crossed the road side by side, her thoughts skittered around in her head... How many couples had made this walk before them up these steps? Couples who'd loved one another so much it hurt.

The sadness that settled over her was so energy-sapping that she went through the introduction process on auto-pilot, not realising until they had moved a little apart from the two men that she had not retained their names.

'Is that your phone?' she asked when Ezio's phone rang, thinking, *for God's sake answer it,* as the trill went on and on.

'Yes, it is,' Ezio said, making no effort to take it out.

'It's stopped.' Realising she sounded relieved, she added politely, 'Perhaps they will ring back.'

'Oh, *they* will,' he intoned grimly.

'You said there would be no press,' she reminded him in a hushed undertone as they approached the third man.

'He isn't press. Jake is here at my request.'

'So you have your own personal photographer?' she joked, then thought the joke could be on her. Plenty of people in his position did like to present a carefully contrived image of their perfect personal life. But for starters she'd have known it, and secondly, to give the devil his due, Ezio did not number vanity among his many faults. And it wasn't as if he could be worried about anyone taking an unflattering photo of him because he had no bad side or bad angle—whichever way you looked at him, he was pretty perfect. *Boringly so,* she told herself without much conviction.

'Jake is doing me a favour.'

'He doesn't look like a friend of yours…but then I don't look like…'

One sable brow lifted to an interrogative angle. 'You don't look like…?'

Her eyes slid from his. 'It's just the window dressing.' Her gesture took in the dress and flowers. 'It feels so fake, so insincere. Wouldn't it be better to keep it low key? Given the circumstances.'

'How much more low-key can you get?' he asked, looking exasperated. 'Two witnesses… Yeah, that is really over the top.'

'Hush, he's coming over,' she hissed. The friend with the camera was strolling towards them, the tools of his trade slung over this shoulder.

Ezio introduced them and the other man responded with a smile and a warm handshake. If he thought the entire marriage thing, and more significantly Ezio's choice of bride, strange, nothing in his manner suggested it.

'So you are still happy to leave the choice to me, Ezio…just want the one distributed?'

Ezio nodded.

'Fair enough, but you know there will be an appetite for more… I think that's just the perfect spot… Hold on a minute; I just want to check out the light…' Eyes narrowed, Jake crossed to the green space opposite.

'Distributed to who, exactly?' Tilda asked when he was out of earshot.

'The usual suspects.'

Tilda didn't have a clue who the usual suspects were.

'Don't worry, Jake can make anyone look good.'

It took Tilda a few seconds and a little gasp of outrage and she rose to the teasing challenge.

'I thought I *did* look good!'

It was true. She was not glossy or polished to within an inch of her life like the women he was normally photographed with—that went without saying. But her hair had been co-operative this morning and the soft, natural air-dried waves that framed her heart-shaped face and fell loose almost to her waist were flattering, and her charity-shop-bargain dress looked good on its one-time outing.

Tilda was all for recycling but she rather doubted she would ever wear it after today. Unlike with a normal wedding, the memories would be ones she'd want to bury, not cherish, which was why she was surprised that Ezio wanted photographic evidence.

But she supposed this was all part of this *narrative control* he wanted.

The upwards sweep of his heavy-lidded gaze from her feet to her face did not reveal if he agreed with her bold self-assessment, but the gleam in his eyes made her shiver.

'Did none of the outfits I sent meet with your approval?'

He *had* noticed. Tilda had been afraid he was going to kick up a fuss about the dress, but then the likelihood of him knowing the contents of the vanload of designer clothes that had arrived on her doorstep was remote. It had probably been a pointless gesture to refuse them but, pointless or not, it had seemed an important point to make. She had lost control of so many things but she was still in charge of her wardrobe.

'I'm sure they were perfect.' *As are you…* Her stomach tightened in self-disgust as she dragged her eyes clear of his sinfully sexy face.

She adopted an amused attitude. 'You make it sound as though you spent hours personally selecting them.'

She knew better than most that this task would have been outsourced. In the early months of her employment, he'd tried to task her with outsourcing a parting gift for one of his ex-lovers, but she had made it clear that she did not consider it fitted in with her job description.

She remembered holding her breath as she'd

waited for his response, wondering if the principle was really worth losing her job over. Now she wouldn't have been surprised by his reaction, but she'd been shocked when after a few moment's consideration he had agreed with her. Now, of course, she knew that he liked a clear delineation between his private and work life.

What was she filed under in his compartmentalised brain now? Perhaps he'd created an entire new box: *Temporary Wife/Seen But Not Heard.*

'Actually, I wouldn't know, I refused to sign for them. I'm not pretending to be something I'm not for you. So sorry if I'm not up to your standard.'

'*Pretend...?* You *are* my wife.' He paused to allow the fact to bed in. 'Or you will be in about ten minutes.'

Shock and fear shot through her body and she stood frozen in a furtive 'fight or flight' pose.

'And as for my standards...' His dark gaze drifted across her face. 'You look very beautiful.'

From a point somewhere over his left shoulder where they had strayed to, her eyes swivelled back to his face, ready to react to the sarcastic smirk she was sure would be painted on his face.

No smirk, but instead there was something in his dark eyes that made her stomach knot.

For a full thirty seconds she stopped breathing, then looked away, pretending the shivery sensation in her pelvis and the tightness in her chest hadn't happened.

'Is that meant to be funny?'

'Get a room, you two.'

Startled, Tilda half-turned to where her brother was standing, scrolling through his phone.

'Just wondering, have I got time to…? I'm half through the next level and Ezio hasn't switched his phone off.'

'No!' she snapped, realising that to the casual on-looker, or her brother, their low-voiced interchange could have looked intimate. Ezio might even have *intended* this to be the case. She glanced towards Ezio, who was indeed on his phone.

'Fair enough, keep your hair on!' Sam sniggered, strolling over to take up a position on the steps with the two witnesses who also had their phones out.

Her brother threw her an injured 'I told you so' look that drew a smile from Tilda.

Jake joined them—or rather, her. Ezio had moved away and was in the midst of what seemed to be an animated conversation.

'I'm sorry I can't stay around for the service but I've got the launch for the charity book later. I can't really be a no-show, I need to press the flesh, and it's all for a good cause. You know I'm really grateful for Ezio's contribution, though it would have been even better if he'd have posed for me.'

She was desperately trying to think of a response that would not give away her total ignorance when Ezio appeared.

'Jake, I think I should warn you that my bride doesn't actually have a clue who you are, but she lives a very sheltered life, and we only allow her out at weekends.'

Tilda shot Ezio a look of simmering dislike and offered her best smile to the other man, who looked more amused than offended.

'I used to work for him, so actually, it was *alternate* weekends.'

'Workaholic?'

'Oh, I can tell you know him well.' Tilda gave a husky laugh.

Ezio found it amusing that his bride seemed not to recognise the man who had not only shot the front cover of *Life* magazine twice but had appeared on it. He watched his friend respond to her warm, sexy laugh. There was something tactile about the throaty sound; he was pretty sure that he was going to have to get used to seeing men react to Tilda, while she remained oblivious to the effect that she had on men. What the hell was wrong with the men she'd dated that she didn't already know how utterly bewitching and sexy she was?

If *he'd* dated her she would sure as hell know! Before this thought could develop, his phone began to vibrate.

'I think that… Sorry, got to take this,' he tacked on, glancing at the screen of his vibrating phone as he moved away.

He returned a few moments later. Jake was hanging on to a smiling Tilda's every word and she looked relaxed, as she didn't with him. Ezio felt something move in his chest.

'Sorry about that.'

'Hope you're going to switch it off for the actual ceremony,' Jake joked.

'Oh, the phone is going to the third person in our marriage.' And that was the best possible option. It was much more likely to be a tall blonde... The depressing thought sent her mood spiraling down to her boots.

'Right, guys, down to business... How about across the road? I mean, shame to waste an orange blossom in full flower, given the circumstances...? Jake smiled, not seeming to notice that Ezio looked distracted. Tilda, who had been reading his face for the past four years, did, and wondered about his phone call, the habit of being his PA being a hard one to break.

'Will you hang onto my glasses for me?' she asked, sliding them off her nose.

'Why?' Ezio asked, looking at her outstretched hand. For a nerve-shredding moment, their glances locked.

'For the photos.'

Her fingers responded reluctantly to the mental instruction to unfold and, careful not to get lost in his stare again, she offered her palm, tensing against the deep little shiver when his fingers brushed the exposed flesh.

'Great bones.' The photographer approved, studying her face with a clinical intensity. 'Classic. I'd love to do a series of portraits of you,' he enthused.

'Had we better get on before the world wakes up?' Ezio intervened drily.

'Sure,' Jake responded as he fell into step beside Tilda, who was walking a few steps behind Ezio. He gave her an eye-roll and a silent whistle.

'I've never seen Ezio jealous before. It must be love… That is, of course it's love…' he tacked on hastily. 'I meant it about the portraits, though,' he added. 'I'll give you a call.'

Embarrassed by his misinterpretation of Ezio's impatience, Tilda gave a weak smile, even though she had zero intention of taking him up on his offer, which she still struggled to take seriously.

As she watched Ezio stride across to where she had previously been left standing alone, she debated mentioning to him that some of his behaviour could be misinterpreted. Before she realised that that had probably been his intention—the burning looks, the little touches and the flashes of possessive annoyance were all part of the act.

Relieved she hadn't made a total fool of herself, she responded to his concern that she was cold with a carefully managed, one-size-fits-all, meaningless smile.

'I'm totally fine. It's so pretty here. You could almost forget that in an hour it will be choked with car fumes.' At the moment there was only the distant buzz of traffic as a constant reminder that they were standing in central London.

'You're going to ruin those shoes.' He was looking down at the pale suede sling-backs, the heels of which were firmly embedded in the damp ground. 'Typical Jake, he'd do anything for a good shot— have you hanging off a cliff if it was a good angle.' Ezio's dark gaze flickers up to meet hers.

Tilda tried to say something but her lips wouldn't respond to instruction. Her eyes were glued to Ezio's and her heart was pounding, the air between them seeming to throb with a sexual pulse that nailed her feet to the floor.

'Right, then,' said the photographer. 'How about you just relax… Great, that's lovely, carry on with *that* look, guys…'

With a tiny gasp, she tore her eyes free and fixed them on the floor, the effort making her chest rise and fall dramatically under the silk.

'I'm up here,' Ezio said, his voice pitched in a sexy, uneven tone deeper than normal. 'But, yes, my shoes are new. Put a bit of effort into it, will you? Pretend I'm someone else and look happy.'

Her head came up with an angry jerk at the soft mockery in his voice, registering as she did the strain in the lines around his mouth that suggested he maybe wasn't quite as relaxed as she had imagined. 'I hate having my photo taken and I *can't* pose… And I'm not that good an actress,' she slung up at him, wishing that she was, that she could pretend he was someone else, someone who didn't make her *ache*.

'Relax!' encouraged the photographer, with no discernible irony that she could detect as he began circling them, snapping away.

If her jaw had been clenched less hard, she might have laughed at the impossible advice.

'You heard what the man said.'

'What? That I have got great bones?' she shot back, self-mockery flavouring her delivery. She was already sick of this. She had not signed anything that said she had to pose and look stupid, and when she could get her breathing sorted she was going to tell Ezio that.

'Right, I think…yes… Now move a little closer… That look of love, guys…'

Something flashed in Ezio's smoky eyes that made her breath catch. Did she stumble or did her knees just give? Thinking about the moment later, she was never sure, but one second she was on her own feet and the next she was plastered up against the warm hardness of a male chest, supported by a band of steel arm that was looped around her waist.

'You all right?'

'Thanks, fine…' Only she wasn't. His free hand had curved around her face, drawing it up to his as he stared at her like a starving man, making her melt from the inside out.

'You *do* have great bones,' he said, feeling ridiculous, because it was something that had taken him four years to realise and Jake, damn him, had recognised it within thirty seconds.

He also recognised that he *wanted* her. But he didn't need her; it seemed important to him to make this distinction.

'Oh, for heaven's sake, will you turn it off?' The heat was everywhere as she fought the urge to melt into him.

'What off?'

She compressed her lips and breathed out heavily through her nostrils. As if he didn't know *exactly* what this was doing to her. The warmth of his breath on her nerve endings caused the air to leave her lungs in one long, sibilant hiss as he cupped her chin.

Tilda had speculated but she'd had no idea what *in love* felt like. But, if it felt anything like this, she doubted it would be so popular, she decided as she fought for breath, horribly more conscious of his sheer male physicality in that moment than she had ever been before.

But then, other than the odd brushed elbow, she had always kept a physical distance from him. It was only now that she realised that that hadn't been accidental, that at some level in her subconscious she had always known that it exposed her to the fact she was a million miles from immune to the raw sensuality of the man who broke hearts for a hobby.

'How many photos does he need?' She gritted her teeth, determined not to lose her grip....

What are you holding on to, Tilda?

Whatever it was, she was about to lose it.

'How long is this going to take? My face is aching from smiling. It's not my fault I can't fake it.' Struggling to bury the sensations bombarding her, she took refuge in anger. 'I told you, I'm not photogenic,' she said, the effort of not trembling making her voice almost inaudible.

'You pretended you were not a woman,' he grated, painfully conscious in that moment how *very* female she was. It was not just the warm scent of her that made his nostrils flare, but the female dip and curve of her soft, trembling body that was no longer hidden under sexless clothes. 'Four years you managed that, so pretend now that you're enjoying yourself. Imagine…'

His voice faded as his imagination kicked in big time. The image in his head collided with the green eyes looking up, and the encouraging remarks being made by Jake, who was circling them while adjusting his lenses, becoming a buzz of irritation that was drowned out by the thud of his heart beat.

Then one thing got through.

'How about a kiss, guys?'

Her glance centred on the sensual outline of his mouth, Tilda swallowed hard. '*I'm not* kissing you because someone tells me to.'

'*No…?*'

'No,' she whispered before, stretching up on tip toe, she grabbed the back of his head yanked his face down until she could reach his lips. 'I'm kissing you because *I* want to.' Want didn't really cover the way she was feeling. Need came close, in a 'need to breathe' sense.

She felt his lips cool under hers. It was the only cool thing. She was drowning in a hot sea of sensation. The world stilled and the crazy, marvellous moment went on and on as she drank in the texture of him, the taste… A tiny shred of sanity crept into her head.

'Oh, God!'

She would have fallen back on her heels had the hand pressed to the small of her back not slid around her waist and dragged her up and into him, while the hand curved around her jaw meant her lips were just at the right angle to allow his mouth to cover them.

The slow, sensuous, expert movement of his mouth across her lips drew a deep groan from somewhere inside her.

Then it was over.

'Oh, guys, that was…' Jake was flicking through the digital images on the screen, looking happy. 'You want I should send my choice over for your approval before I distribute them?'

Ezio locked the animal groan that ached to escape in his chest and exhaled through flared nostrils.

'No, we'll leave it to you.'

Ezio looked so cool that she hated him in that moment. All she wanted to do was dissolve into an embarrassed pool of misery on the floor when she thought about how she must have looked, grabbing him. How good it had felt to grab him, to press her breasts up against... She tensed, blinked hard and locked the door on this line of thought.

Tilda nodded at the photographer, who was making his apologies as he gathered his gear and headed for a vintage sports car parked a little way down the street.

Digging deep, she adopted a coolness she was several universes away from feeling. 'Well, at least that part is over with.' Just the actual wedding to go... She refused to think beyond it.

Over with...

Ezio glanced down at her, thinking she was right—she was a very bad actress—and she was wrong—it had barely even begun.

The innate carnality of her kiss had wiped away any self-delusion he had managed to retain that he was in control... He wasn't. He wasn't even sure he wanted to be.

He was about to marry a woman who kissed like a wanton, hungry angel and liked to be in control. He could work with that.

CHAPTER FIVE

WHEN THEY STEPPED out of the building it was not to a shower of rose petals and cheers but the distant sound of bad-tempered car horns.

While they'd been inside the sun had vanished, blocked by heavy grey cloud. Fine drizzle that was falling steadily had darkened the pavements and the sound of the steady stream of traffic moving past drowned out the bird song.

Shouldn't she be feeling different…? Tilda didn't know how or what she was feeling, but it wasn't married.

She risked a quick glance up at the man beside her, the uniform grey of their surroundings emphasising his vibrant warmth of bronze colouring.

He didn't appear to be feeling the chill that made her hunch her shoulders in an effort to retain some heat as she hovered just inside the shelter offered by the enclosed porch.

His eyes touched hers, a question in the dark

depths. 'Are you OK?' Her green stare had a glazed quality that brought a frown to his brow.

Tilda gave a shrug. 'I'm fine.'

Before he could respond to her unconvincing claim, his phone began to ring, he glanced at the screen and swore. 'Sorry. I need to take this.'

Of course you do, she thought. *Welcome to the rest of your life, Tilda—or at least the next six months.*

Jogging down the steps, Sam paused beside her as Ezio stepped out into the drizzle.

'Are you changing your name?'

'I haven't even thought about it,' she admitted but now she thought it was hardly worth the bother for six months.

'I don't mind if you do, you know…it makes sense he's famous and you're not.'

Well, that was inarguable.

The damp had already penetrated the thin fabric of her dress halfway to the limo when someone appeared carrying a massive umbrella. Under its shelter she reached the kerb, where the open-doored limo waited.

Glancing over her shoulder, she saw that Ezio still had his phone at his ear. He lifted it away briefly to respond to something Sam had said with a nod of assent.

'I'm riding upfront, I don't want to be a gooseberry!' Sam yelled, jogging past her and around the limo.

'You don't have to—' Her words were lost in the slamming of the door.

She slid in, adjusting her dress before the door was closed, immediately muffling the noise of the traffic which, despite the early hour, had built up to rush hour level. Smoothing the skirt over her thighs, the ring on her finger caught the light. She paused and looked at the gold band that lay snugly against the big square-cut emerald.

She was still staring at it when Ezio slid in beside her. 'You're trying to figure out if they're real. You've found me out.' He held his hands up in mock surrender. 'They're paste. I'm a cheapskate.'

'I wish they were! I don't feel comfortable walking around with a fortune on my finger.'

He stared at her for a moment and loosed a laugh. 'You are a very unusual woman, you know that?'

It was hard to tell from his expression if that was a good thing or a bad thing.

'What are you doing?' She nodded towards his phone.

'Switching it off... Oh, the storm has shifted its path, so there's no issue with the flight—got the news update just before we went in.'

'Good about the storm... Actually, I didn't know there was a storm.' Though, now that she thought about it, Saul had mentioned something about the weather during the phone call last night.

Saul was actually being extremely helpful. He'd looked over her mission statement, suggested a couple of tweaks and given her the names of some potential trustees.

'It's been on every news bulletin for the last forty-eight hours. The phone…' He hesitated before volunteering, 'My father has been ringing me non-stop since last night.'

'Your father?'

'You sound surprised,' he observed, tucking the phone in his pocket. The gesture was an empty one. He might want to take a break from his father, but it was not practical to cut himself off entirely. His fantasy version of a desert island was a week with his phone switched off—the desert island scenario stood more chance of actually happening.

Tilda conceded the point with a faint shrug. 'I suppose I had the impression that you weren't particularly close.' It wasn't so much what he'd said about his father but the fact he rarely mentioned him at all.

'You had the right impression, so don't worry, there will be no dutiful visit for you to endure,' he drawled. 'We do the yearly dinner, though my mother and I do meet up through the year.'

Tilda, who remembered the dates being in his diary, didn't say anything. 'I wasn't thinking about that. I… Oh…' His meaning suddenly hit her and she felt stupid for being so slow. 'You mean that by then we will be divorced,' she said tonelessly.

In the act of sliding one arm along the back of the seat, he paused, something flickering in his dark eyes. 'I suppose we will be.'

'Has your father found out about the wedding? Was he angry?'

'My father does not have the right to be angry. If he knows we are married, I haven't told him.' She sensed a tension in his steely posture underneath his languid pose. 'Actually, my mother has left him… about thirty years too late, in my opinion, but she has.' He cast a knowing look over her face. 'Yes, it was an affair, or rather the last in a long list of affairs… As it turns out, one too many.'

'Oh.'

'He wanted to know if I know where she is. The man is falling apart,' he said, sounding not too unhappy about this.

'And do you? Know where she is?'

He rolled his neck, as if to the relieve the tension lying in his broad shoulders. 'Yes.'

'But you wouldn't tell him.'

He produced a wry smile and shook his head. 'I'd pay good money to see him crawl to beg her to come back…bare foot and hot coals involved in the equation works for me too….but I gave my word. And it will do him good to think she is with another man…which of course he does, because he judges everyone by his own particularly low standards.' He sneered, his mouth thinning in contempt. 'I'm not claiming mine are high, but at least I have enough self-awareness to recognise the traits I share with the bastard. I might have screwed around, but at least I never hurt anyone doing it.'

Despite the headlines about him, she realised that it was true—if he used women, they used him right back. And who could blame them? she thought, her eyes drifting to his irresistible mouth.

'Is that why you never got married?' she blurted, hastily averting her eyes.

In the act of running his finger around his collar, he paused, an expression she could not interpret sliding across his face as the silence stretched so long she thought he was not going to respond.

'In that way at least I differ from my father. I know I'm selfish, but I'd never put a woman I *half*-liked, let alone one I professed to love, through the sort of humiliation my mother has suffered.'

'You married me,' she said in a small voice.

He jolted in his seat, a look of contrition spreading across his face. 'Oh, Tilda, I...'

She gave a brittle little laugh. 'Oh, don't be daft, it's fine. I know our marriage is not the same and, heavens, *love* doesn't come into it.' She laughed again, ignoring the bleakness that had invaded her heart... *Think about that later.*

Or maybe not. Some things were better left.

Aware of his forensic scrutiny, she painted a look onto her face that suggested curiosity rather than hurt feelings. 'So where is your mother? Or am I not in the need-to-know loop?' He seemed to juggle a lot of loops; perhaps his right hand actually *didn't* know what his left was doing, though she knew better. He had a mind like a steel trap and, to use a chess analogy her brother would approve of, he was always thinking three moves ahead.

'She's taken an apartment in Paris and had enrolled on a post-graduate degree in Fine Art at the Sorbonne. I hope she does meet someone who appreciates her.' He sank his head into the leather head support and turned to look at her.

'I am not enough of a bastard to spend my wedding day on the phone to my lover.' But bastard enough to know that was what she had been thinking, he thought, self-disgust tightening like a fist in his belly at the recognition. And he'd let her carry on thinking it, just because he didn't like explaining himself to anyone.

'I was getting mad,' she admitted. 'It seemed… *rude*.' She wasn't asking for much, but basic good manners seemed a not unreasonable ask to her.

'It seemed…rude…' he echoed with a half-smile, thinking that her mouth was not made for looking prim. The attempt was sexy, though. 'How will I cope in the office without you to tell me when I'm out of line?'

Her emerald eyes flew wide. 'I… I never did, I just…'

'Suggested it…?'

'Subtly.'

One corner of his mouth lifted but his eyes… The expression glittering deep in the obsidian depths made her think of his mouth feathering across her lips… As the thought progressed, her breathing grew faster and shorter before she literally shook it away and pushed out a breathy observation. 'You know you're going to have to turn your phone on, don't you?'

'I know. I might block my father, though.'

'Ezio, you can't do that! What if there was an emergency?'

Ezio snorted, his fingers tapping the wooden armrest impatiently. 'This traffic is…' As he was speaking, the traffic started to move.

'It heard you and got scared.'

A half-smile glimmered as he leaned back into his seat and, loosening the knot on his silk tie, stretched his legs out.

'Lucky we settled on pre-wedding photos; it's really bucketing down now.'

Tilda flashed him a look and was tempted to point out that *she* hadn't decided on anything, but she didn't want to break the little lull in tension they were enjoying.

He patted his pocket and pulled out her new glasses. 'I forgot… You need these?'

'Oh, I forgot.' She was shocked by the admission. Not long ago the idea of appearing without glasses would have made her feel naked; they had been part of her persona for so long. 'Thanks.'

Ezio didn't immediately hand them over, instead he held them out, regarding them through narrowed eyes. 'Very pretty,' he decided, before his gaze shifted to Tilda.

For a split second she thought about telling him the truth but held back. This was *her* makeover, not his.

The difference was important to her and, she realised now, was part of the reason she had refused the delivery of designer outfits. Tilda had no ambition to be some sort of Cinderella. She was nobody's project, she was her own woman.

'No tints?' he observed.

She shook her head. 'I liked this pair.' And she had rationalised her purchase by telling herself that specs were a fashion accessory.

'Just *how* short-sighted are you?' He held them out, and for a split second she thought he was about to raise them to his own eyes.

'I can honestly say that the wedding was a blur.' It was true, just not in the way he thought she meant. 'In fact, this entire day feels surreal.' Maybe she would wake up any moment and say, *I had this really vivid dream.* She turned her head to look him in the face. 'Sorry for moaning…you hate this as much as me.'

'Oh, not *that* much,' he said drily, the irony not lost on him. 'You know, there are some women who might consider marrying me not a total waste of a day.'

Tell me something I don't know, she thought.

'Sorry, it's nothing personal—and I'll make the best of it, I promise. I'm not a whiner,' she added solemnly, in case he thought she was going to bleat

about it constantly. 'I'm a realist. I know you made
a better boss than you will a husband.'

'You thought I was a good boss?'

While it was noticeable he hadn't concurred with
her initial statement, if she hadn't known that Ezio
didn't need approval from anyone she'd have thought
her admission had pleased him.

'No woman ever had to push through a glass ceiling, because you never had one—that's rare.'

'Thank you. I'm glad you think I'm an equal op-
portunities employer, but actually I just like to re-
ward talent. And, like the man says, if you've not
tried it yet, don't knock it. I might be an exceptional
husband.'

Tilda, who fully expected him to be an absent
husband, didn't respond to the teasing.

'I know today hasn't been easy, but the next six
months don't have to be unadulterated misery.'

'Why, because I've married a sex god?' The moment the waspish words left her lips, she would have
given anything to retract them. 'It's that damned article—and don't say you don't know *what* article.'
Colour rose to her face as she remembered reading
the kiss-and-tell article that had been liberally sprin-
kled with lurid details.

'I don't, but I intend to look for it now.'

Her cheeks were burning but she made a recovery and managed a disdainful sniff. 'I'll send you
the link. But, although a lot of the comments thought

she was just after some publicity, even allowing for a bit of exaggeration, I'm sure you're great in bed!'

A gleam of appreciation appeared in his eyes. 'You look like Matilda on a Monday morning, looking disapproving because I've done something wrong.'

'It's still me. Just think of me as the piece of office furniture who can talk back outside the office,' she snapped back, pretending not to be aware that he'd shifted his position and his thigh was now against her own.

It was a lot of pretending!

Irritated with herself for being aware, she blamed that kiss… It had made her feel excited, vulnerable, a dozen other things she couldn't put a name to when she thought of it. Thought of the taste of him, thought of the tangle of tongues, the feeling… *Oh, God!*

'What is it?'

She shook her head. Then, desperate to divert attention from her momentary blip, she glanced pointedly at Sam, whose head was nodding away to the music he was listening to via the ear buds pushed in his ears. The glass screen protected her from the audible boom of bass she knew would be pumping out, despite the headphones. She felt a stab of sympathy for the driver and hoped the poor man shared Sam's taste in music.

'He'll probably be stone deaf by the time he's twenty.' *And I'll be a divorcee.* But divorce was six months away and, thinking of that kiss…would she ever stop thinking of it?…six months suddenly seemed a very long time.

She'd jumped in without thinking this thing through. In her defence, she had worked closely with him for four years. She'd have thought if incapacitating lust was going to be a problem it would have reared its ugly head by now.

She took a calming deep breath. This would work…this had to work… She owed it to Sam and she owed it to her parents, and the silent vow she had made to them at the funeral.

She didn't have to enjoy the next six months, she just had to get through them. The logical part of her brain told her she should not have leapt before taking precautions, such as having her own lawyer go through the contract she had signed, or working out that Ezio should come with a 'once kissed never forgotten' warning.

But all it took was for the image of Sam lying in that hospital bed to come into her head and the knowledge that the next time he might not be so lucky…that the next time, he might end up with a criminal record that could blight his entire life before it had started…and she knew it didn't matter. She'd have done it anyway.

Ezio's voice made her start, which was ridiculous, because she really hadn't forgotten he was there. He didn't have a forgettable bone in his perfect body.

She turned her head slowly, delaying the moment their eyes made contact. He'd dominate an auditorium, let alone the plush, air-conditioned interior of a luxury limo. Maybe the air-conditioning wasn't working, or maybe it was her own air-conditioning… because, even though she felt hot, she was shivering.

Her green eyes had a bruised, almost blank quality. She looked so young…much younger than her years.

'You have something against those flowers?' Concern roughened his voice.

She looked from his face to the drooping flowers she had picked up in her white-knuckled hands, as if she couldn't even remember picking them up.

'Or are they a substitute for who you really want to strangle? I think the technical term for that hold is a death grip.'

Ezio watched as she released the choke-hold on the ribbon-tied posy and put them down on the seat between them. The flowers looked almost as sad and wilted as she did. Her heart-shaped face made him think of a flower, her graceful neck the stem that held it up.

He rejected the image. Tilda was tough and resilient. He had always admired the fact that she always rose to a challenge, she kept her head and did not respond emotionally—it was one of the reasons that he had stopped looking for a replacement.

His long-term PA Angela's departure had been sudden after she'd fallen ill, but she had been the one who'd recommended her assistant, asking him to give her a chance. '*She'll shine*,' she'd said.

Ezio hadn't imagined the scared creature whose main skill had seemed to be the perfection of the art of fading into the background shining, not even in a quiet way, but he'd humoured Angela. Typically, she'd felt guilty for leaving him in the lurch, and he had never anticipated the situation would become permanent. But it turned out that Matilda Raven had only been quiet because she'd been learning and, before he realised it, she had made herself an invaluable asset.

He remembered the first time she had stood up to him. He could see her now, standing there looking at him and saying quite calmly, 'I think that's a really bad idea.'

To say he'd been astonished was an understatement.

He had tried to remember the last time anyone had told him *any* idea he'd had was bad…and couldn't. He'd complained about boot-lickers but then, when he'd encountered someone who wasn't inclined to polish his ego, his first reaction had been to annihilate her verbally…and then he'd remembered someone, probably him, saying that if ideas were not open to challenge there was no progress.

So, instead of yelling, he'd sat on the edge of his desk and thrown out his challenge.

'So, tell me, *why* do you think this is a bad idea?'

She had, calmly and concisely, and when he'd asked her what she would have done she'd told him that too. A lot of those suggestions had been unworkable but there'd been a kernel of possibility in several.

That was the day their relationship had changed and, while he'd missed Angela, he'd got over it. But he'd missed Tilda's presence in his office more than he would have imagined. She was here in his life now, though, still provoking and challenging him.

For six months.

The glass partition between the front and passenger seat suddenly slid down.

'Phillip.' Sam nodded at the driver. 'He says we're here.'

'The clue is the sign and the planes,' Ezio retorted drily.

'I've never flown before, you know—well, I have, but I was small, and I know only because there are photos, and Tilda tells me I threw up all over Mum on the plane and it stank.'

'Well, I sincerely hope that you do not throw up on this flight.'

'I've been reading about jet propulsion and—'

'I hope you haven't been making a nuisance of yourself, Sam?' Tilda was worried.

'Of course not. Phillip was interested.'

'*Phillip* was a captive audience, and he is polite. I had the foresight to pack the parachutes.'

Tilda tensed and half-closed her eyes.

Sam could get defensive at even the slightest hint of mockery—probably because he had suffered merciless teasing at school over the years, despite his often dry sense of humour.

But, after a pause, Sam laughed.

If *she'd* have said that, he'd have sulked for a week!

CHAPTER SIX

ONE OF THE experiences Tilda wanted to take away from her short stint as a billionaire's bride was that of getting to fly in a private jet. Once would do; she had travelled on the odd occasion with Ezio, but never outside the UK.

She had seen Angelos private jets with the discreet gold logo on the runway on several occasions when Ezio had requested she meet him at the airport to fill him in personally on the way to a meeting.

She'd often speculated what they looked like inside, and the luxury and space in the private jet was not a let-down. While Sam was trying to con himself a place up front with the pilots, she took a seat. Baggage allowances were not an issue but Tilda had brought on board a small carry-on containing some fresh clothes.

She intended to enjoy the novelty of using the on-board shower room facilities, which she knew existed, because she'd asked about Ezio's wet hair on one of the occasions she'd met him coming off a flight.

An image flashed into her head of him immaculately suited and booted, his dark hair slicked back, striding through the foyer towards her, drawing every single eye in the place and seemingly totally oblivious to the fact.

She pushed away the image and didn't try to stifle her yawn, partly to prove to herself how relaxed she was, but mostly because the tensions of the day were catching up with her and the creeping exhaustion was enveloping her like a blanket.

She stretched out her legs and pushed her shoulder blades into the seat, only to reverse the process abruptly and sit bolt upright when an attendant appeared with champagne in a bucket and two glasses. She nodded her thanks and smiled at him, wondering if this was simply normal practice when Ezio travelled with a woman, though she doubted many of Ezio's travel companions had come with a teenage boy in tow.

A drink was either a very bad idea or a very good idea but, as she sat there staring at the bottle, she decided that, bad or good, she was going to say yes… It had been a long day and it wasn't even lunchtime yet.

'Wh-what…? Wh-where…?'

Ezio glanced up as a deep sigh left Tilda's parted lips, her lashes fluttering like butterflies against her lightly flushed cheeks as her luminous green eyes opened. Her eyes darted back and forth, the unfamiliar surroundings deepening her panic until she encountered a face that anchored her.

'It's you…' She studied Ezio's starkly beautiful face and smiled.

Ezio caught his breath at the invitation glowing in her eyes. His physical response was instant and painful. Her mouth was just the most… He had no idea where he got the strength not to accept the invitation in those incredible eyes. He could feel his sense of time and place fade fast, along with his resistance, as she lifted a fluttering hand towards his cheek. His chest was heaving as he struggled to draw in oxygen through flared nostrils and he felt his control slipping through his fingers like sand grains.

Their mouths were inches apart when, just as unexpectedly as it had been offered, the invite was withdrawn, a light seemed to switch on in her head and the slumberous promise went cold.

He remained hot.

She sat bolt-upright, almost knocking heads with him.

Ezio straightened up in pain.

Theos… If Tilda ever learnt the power those eyes had, no man would be safe.

What man would want to be *safe*…? What was safety compared to the lush promise of the lips?

The thought surfaced out of nothing, or at least deep frustration, and once there fed on the oxygen of his need. Packing it away would take more focus than he could tap into at that actual moment so it stayed there at the back of his thoughts, bedding down, inviting him to rationalise the needs he was denying…asking *why*?

He focused on the *why nots*. It was not a cold shower but it was all he had.

How about we have great sex for six weeks but then what for the rest of the six months…? Sure, that is really a good idea.

How about six months isn't enough…? Tilda was not like any of the women who had drifted in and out of his life leaving no ripples in its smooth, efficient running.

What if he hurt her? There was no *if* about it. He was enough like his father to know that he would. This argument with himself was the clincher. He might be selfish but he was already using her, but to hurt her… He felt the rejection of that at a cellular level.

'We're here—why didn't you wake me?' It was less a question and more an accusation.

'You were exhausted and it's been a long day.'

'You snore.' This was Sam, who walked down the aisle with a back pack slung over this shoulder. Presumably his suit was crushed in it, as he'd changed into a pair of khaki chinos and a tee shirt. His comfort made Tilda aware that she wasn't at all comfortable—she was wearing a dress she had slept in, which no doubt looked it.

'Thank you, brother dear, I love you too,' she responded with a grin.

'I wanted to wake you but he wouldn't let me.'

'You do not snore… Drool a little…?'

'When did you become a double act?' A smile appeared in Tilda's eyes as she looked from one to the other and some of the tension slid from her shoulders. She was actually starting to feel a bit ridiculous for getting worked up about a searing, hot, hungry look when it had been a product of her sleeping subconscious.

It was connected to reality by her guilt, which was irrational. A person could not be held responsible for their subconscious, it was not real, but the *not real* had left the echo of it low in her belly in an ache of carnal yearning.

In the real world she was not yearning she was… A tiny pucker appeared between her feathery dark brows. She felt creased and crumpled, much like the old dish rag her dress probably resembled by now—a dish rag that had been slept in.

Rubbing away the frown between her eyes, she lifted her heavy, silky hair off her neck. The plan had been to tie it back before they landed.

Why was she worrying? There was no one to impress except… Actually, there was no need to impress Ezio, which was just as well; outside the office she wouldn't have known where to begin.

And she definitely wasn't going try and look stupid making the effort. Mouth set firm, she unclipped her belt and rose to her feet, shaking out the silky strands of hair as she did so.

She felt Ezio's eyes on her and turned her head, catching *something* in his eyes—a trick of the light, maybe. It was only there for a split second. Imagination or not, she was wide awake now, all her senses tingling, her stomach somersaulting.

'Am I holding everyone up? Sorry, I didn't sleep much last night.'

'I hope he wasn't a nuisance?' she said anxiously.

'I would tell him if he was,' Ezio responded with a deadpan look that broke into a grin as he added, 'Relax, he was fine. He ate a great deal… I had forgotten that teenage boys are never full. But fortunately, under the circumstances, he was not sick at all.'

'You don't know what you missed. There is a *chef* on board.'

'I'm sure you'll tell me what I missed.' Tilda put a hand to the back of her neck and rotated her shoulders to alleviate the burning ache of tension that had already taken up residence between her shoulder blades.

Push through the pain, she thought ruefully as she picked up her bag. 'I meant to change.'

Ezio's glance travelled from her feet to the top of her shiny head before he casually claimed her bag.

'I'm fine.' Her grip tightened on the handle and her jaw squared, the resistance only lasting a second before it occurred to her that disputing everything would leave her with little energy for the fights that really mattered. The ones that she was starting to think were inevitable.

'Thank you.' She forced the words out as she relinquished her bag.

He tipped his dark, glossy head in sardonic acknowledgment. 'You look fine like that.' The throw away remark was delivered with no particular expression, and his eyes were hidden by the fringe of his lashes, but the tension she sensed in him made her stomach lurch.

She hurried to fill the static silence before it became impenetrable. 'I feel a bit creased and...' She broke off as his eyes met hers.

'You look beautiful. Accept a compliment with grace, Tilda.'

She fought the temptation to look back over her shoulder and carried on walking, making damn sure she didn't stumble. Because it wasn't the compliment, it was the source it came from, that had her feeling very unsteady.

Her reaction to his formidable physical presence was a problem, but all she had to do was sit tight and wait... She knew his schedule—Ezio rarely spent more than three days a month in the Athens office, and on those occasions he sometimes flew back the same day.

She noticed that Sam seemed quite subdued as they went through the tedious but VIP-accelerated airport formalities. Her anxiety was mixed with guilt. This was happening because she wanted to prioritise Sam, but yet again it was Ezio who occupied her thoughts…and not in a way she had ever imagined.

The problem was she was imagining too much.

'Are you OK?' she asked, lightly throwing an arm around her brother's shoulders.

Just ahead a senior official of some sort had attached himself to Ezio's side. She knew his attentive attitude would not be to Ezio's taste, but what he liked or did not like was not for her to worry about. She found herself hoping uncharitably that the man was boring the pants off Ezio.

'Fine. Actually, if you must know, I'm regretting the last burger…' Sam admitted, pressing his stomach. 'But I mean, a chef and food on tap… I asked and no one said no.' He gave a '*go figure*' eye-roll of wonder. 'It was like a dream.'

Tilda's lips twitched. Sam dreamt of an endless supply of fried food and she dreamt of… Well, who was she to criticise?

'It didn't occur to you to say no?'

'I did but two burgers too late.'

The official peeled away before they reached a sparsely occupied private parking area. Ezio was speaking with a group of airport staff who were in the process of putting luggage in the boot of large shiny four-wheel drive with blacked-out windows.

It looked showroom-new. Tilda glanced at her brother, who was still looking interestingly pale.

'If you're going to be sick…'

'Got it covered. I'll open the window.'

Tilda grimaced. 'Thanks for that image.' And she watched as her brother climbed into the back seat. Ah well, if he did spoil the leather upholstery it would serve Ezio right for not realising that a teenage boy had to be told when he had had enough to eat.

'You worry too much.' He had not intended to say it but she looked so… Did the woman never put herself first?

'Do I?'

'About Sam.' He'd noticed Sam trudging along looking sorry for himself and, having seen the boy keep the on-board chef on his toes, he was not particularly surprised or concerned. It was the worried looks floating in Sam's direction that he somehow couldn't filter out.

Her raised brows went higher, her delicate nostrils quivery with the effort of not responding.

Her restraint lasted a good ten seconds before, with a smile heavy with sarcasm, she bit back through gritted teeth, 'I bow to your superior knowledge on the subject.'

'I watched him munch his way through half a cow, and I happen to know quite a lot about unrestrained indulgence.'

'I'm sure you do, but spare me the details of your sexual endurance.'

Laughter burst from his lips.

A drop-dead look was not quite as effective as she'd have liked when she knew her face was scarlet but she gave it a shot anyway. 'And, if you watched, why on earth didn't you stop him?'

'In my experience, saving people from their mistakes is less effective than letting them suffer the results. You only stick your hand in the fire once...' His eyes fell to her lips and he immediately felt the painful evidence that this was not always true; sometimes those flames were just too tempting.

'Well, I wouldn't know. I am not drawn to flames, and anyway, that is the most stupid thing I have ever heard!' she exclaimed with a scornful sniff. 'What would you do, let a toddler stumble into the path of an oncoming car to show that being hit by a big chunk of metal going at thirty miles an hour really hurts?' She snorted. 'Tough love is another way of saying "I don't give a damn"!'

She broke off, breathless after her impassioned outburst. Every inch of her slender, supple body was vibrating with outrage that had fired up out of nothing, basically. Things seemed to overheat at a very low temperature between them but, *Theos*, she was quite magnificent... He had never been with a woman who aroused him this much.

He had never been with her.

He stood there wishing that he could go back to a point in time when he could have confidently tossed back that he didn't give a damn and did not care what hurt his words caused.

That ship has sailed, mocked the sardonic voice in his head.

'Fine. I spoke out of turn.'

The sparkle of disdain faded from her eyes, replaced by surprise. Perversely, the instant he stopped defending himself, she wanted to make excuses for him.

'And I overreacted a bit,' she admitted. 'It's my job to worry about Sam. I don't always do such a great job and…well…it's been the two of us for so long…' She broke off, thinking it still *was* the two of them. 'And his life is changing so much he's bound to struggle.'

'Sam seems to be coping. He seemed resilient.'

'He's had to be. When Mum and Dad died, for a long time afterwards he had terrible night terrors. He'd wake up in the night screaming.'

Watching her face, Ezio wondered if Sam was the only one who'd had night terrors.

'He used to ask me if I was going to die and leave him too.' She gulped unshed tears, roughing the edges of her disclosure. 'He had some grief counselling…we both did,' she said quietly. 'But I get scared sometimes. When things seem fine it all goes…' She gave a helpless little shrug.

'These boys he got mixed up with…?'

She nodded. 'He's sensible really, but he so desperately wants to belong…'

Her green eyes sought his for understanding

and that look made him feel as though a hand had reached in his chest and squeezed.

When he'd been nailing the fine detail, treating this marriage like any other contract, he had failed to appreciate that even a temporary marriage would impact his life, especially one that came with a ready-made family… At least, not in the way it was. Just considering someone other than himself was a mind-bending change for him.

'You're very kind to Sam, and I'm grateful. He likes you.' She really hadn't anticipated Ezio becoming some sort of role model for her brother. 'It worries me…' she admitted.

'What worries you, Tilda?' It worried him that the sight of her nibbling nervously at her lush lower lips was exerting such fascination, and that the impulse to wrap her in his arms and tell her everything would be all right was growing more compelling by the second. 'Surely,' he added brusquely, 'It is good that he likes me?'

She nodded and cast a furtive look over her shoulder. 'Of course, but he doesn't know that this is… well, not real…temporary. I'm afraid he'll get *too* fond of you.'

'I wouldn't hurt Sam.'

Her eyes flew to his face. 'I know you wouldn't mean to.'

'There is no reason we can't stay in touch *after.*'

'Stay in touch with Sam?' She was startled by the idea.

'I meant…' In all honesty, he didn't have a clue what he meant. 'People remain friends after divorces.'

'But they were friends before, we are…'

'Not friends,' he supplied, a hard edge to his voice.

'I wasn't going to say that.' Even if it was true. 'We were, I suppose, well, *nothing* outside the office.'

'So is the enforced intimacy making you feel uncomfortable?'

She felt a sudden spurt of panic as his glance connected. 'There is no intimacy, enforced or otherwise. We aren't strangers but I don't *know* you…' He was constantly challenging her pre-conceptions in a way that meant she couldn't relax. 'Not in any sense of…' Her eyes slid from his dark, sardonic stare. 'For instance, I never realised that you didn't travel with security in Greece.'

His lips quirked at the obvious attempt to change the subject. 'I travel with security most places…visible if you want to draw attention, and less visible…' She watched as he lifted a hand, turned to his right and a car fifty yards away flashed its lights. He then turned left and the same thing happened before he swivelled back to Tilda. 'If you don't. You are perfectly safe. I would never allow anything to happen to you or Sam.'

'I wasn't worried, just surprised.'

'The moment we got married, you and Sam became potential kidnap targets.'

'Kidnap…?' She cast a glance at Sam in the back seat and shuddered. *Kidnap*. The word floated through her head, sounding more sinister with each repetition. It wasn't just the word it was the matter-of-fact way he'd said it. 'I'm stupid, I didn't think…'

'Why should you think?' The stricken look on her face felt like a stab in his chest. 'This is not *your* normal, it is mine.' He gestured to the waiting cars, then placed a hand flat on the black paintwork of the gleaming monster they stood beside. 'Armour-plated cars with bullet-proof glass are my world, and while you are in it you will be safe. I swear on my life.'

'I know, I never thought otherwise… I trust you.'

His lashes came down like a veil but Tilda sensed another mercurial shift his mood.

'Well, if you are ready?'

He held the door open, holding out a hand to help her on the step.

'Thanks,' she murmured, not looking at him, afraid that contact with his dark eyes would shake loose the confusing cocktail of dangerous emotions swirling inside her. She could not predict which one it would be, but none would be relaxing.

CHAPTER SEVEN

SAM SEEMED TO regain form as they drove through the dust and congestion of the city, Ezio good-naturedly answering his constant flow of questions while negotiating the traffic, which in itself deserved a medal.

After they had been driving thirty minutes or so, the urban sprawl gave way to a quieter area. The streets they drove along were lined with palms and the sea, which she had only glimpsed at a distance through concrete, was now a dazzling blue backdrop against the beaches that lay along the bay.

'This is so pretty.'

'Vouliagmeni,' he said with a nod.

'Sorry, you must feel like a tour guide.'

'Familiarity breeds contempt. It is actually good to see these places anew through the eyes of visitors.'

The small smile curving her lips faded at the reminder of her status…*visitors*.

Oblivious to her abrupt change of mood, he expanded. 'Many well-heeled Athenians come here.

There is a thermal lake and people bathe there even in the winter. I will take you there.'

'Before I leave, you mean?'

'Who's leaving?'

Tilda felt a stab of guilty panic.

'Are you looking forward to the school tour tomorrow, Sam?'

Successfully diverted, Sam earnestly began to discuss in detail with Ezio the computer facilities, which he couldn't believe were as good as the prospectus suggested. He was also extremely impressed by the calibre of some of the staff, many of whom had come to teaching from a diverse spread of interest and expertise.

'How much farther to go?' she asked during a lull in the conversation.

They had left behind the pretty beachside town fifteen minutes ago and turned off through two massive wrought-iron gates onto a private road. The loops, dips and sharp inclines meant they quickly lost sight of the lead vehicle, though occasionally they got a glimpse of a dust cloud. The one bringing up the rear hung back, putting more distance between them.

'You wanted to know *when*? Ten, nine…'

In the back seat, Sam joined in.

Tilda folded her arms across her chest. Did men ever grow up? 'With this sort of build-up…' she began. 'Oh, my God!'

Ezio brought the four-wheel-drive to a halt. The

pause meant the blacked-out limo that had been following them came to halt too further down the road.

'Villa Amphitrite.'

'The goddess of the sea,' Sam said. 'Well, you can see why.'

She really could! Set in the midst of formal gardens that stretched down to the sea, with a mountain backdrop looking out over it, the dramatic main structure was snow-white, including the roof, it seemed, giving the impression it was floating above the sea like a cloud.

There appeared to be two adjacent wings. One had a soft blue tinge and a square tower that stood in one corner looked gold at this distance.

'That,' Tilda breathed, unable to take her eyes off the spectacular sight, 'Is not what I was expecting. When you said "villa" I was thinking something… I don't know…less palatial, more rustic, with maybe a pool. Less historical ancient…more old.'

'The original building was ancient but that fell into ruin many years ago. Some ancestor of mine bought the ruin because he liked the view.'

'He knew a good view when he saw one.'

'He was full of good intentions, so the family legend goes, the "mouth not action" type. He'd inherited money, so basically he just sat, looked at the view and drank a little—actually, a lot, by all accounts. By the time his equally languid sons had died, the place was a wreck and half the land that came with it was sold off.'

Well, nobody could say that Ezio had inherited the lazy gene! It was impossible to imagine his combustible energy ever slowing enough to allow him to relax, let alone laze.

'It passed to my grandfather.'

'And he was not lazy.'

Ezio's white grin flashed. 'No, that was the last thing you could call him.'

'Well, it's…' She threw up her hands, genuinely lost for words. 'I don't know how you can bear to leave it? If I…' She stopped, her eyes widening in self-reproachful dismay. She had almost done it again. It was only luck that Sam had stepped outside to take a million photos on his phone.

'We should be careful, Ezio, with Sam…'

'So what is your plan with Sam, so that we are reading from the same page when the time comes to tell him?'

'When that time comes, I'm hoping that he won't need telling. I know in some ways he's pretty immature for his age but in others… He'll pick up on the clues. I'm not saying he knows much about people in love but I think he'll soon cotton on that we aren't.'

'And do you know a lot about people in love, Tilda?'

'More than Sam,' she countered carefully.

'From experience?'

She felt the anger move like a rash of prickly heat across her skin. 'I'd say that's none of your business. What are you smiling about?' she tacked on crankily.

'I was wondering how many times in the office you wanted to say that to me.'

'It *was* your business then, that is the difference—though if you'd have asked me that back then I'd have still said it was none of your business and punched you regardless.'

Ezio threw back his head and laughed.

'One of Tilda's jokes?' Sam said, climbing back in and waggling his eyebrows at Tilda as he teased her. 'He's only being polite because you're on your honeymoon.'

Honeymoon? 'We're not—'

'We're not going away at the moment. We're waiting until I can take a decent stretch of time off, though we might island-hop for the odd weekend. I have a boat.'

'Big super-yacht?'

'No, a sailing boat—a thirty-footer, cross-over cruiser-racer, comfortable but built for speed. She's a beauty.'

If this was an invention it was a good one. His enthusiasm sounded genuine but Tilda didn't actually remember any photos of his model-clone girlfriends lounging half-naked on a sailing boat of any size. For that matter, she had never seen any of them at Villa Amphitrite.

Her eyes flicked to the villa. It looked almost unreal from here.

'You ready?'

She had felt his stare but she hadn't turned her

head and she still didn't. The answer to his question was a loud no, on *so* many levels.

'Yes. It looks original from here.'

'From this angle at this distance, yes; you'll see what I mean when we're down there. It is definitely not a legitimate restoration, but a lot of the original features have been incorporated into the fabric of the new building. According to family legend, Amphitrite is named for the temple to her that the white marble for the original building was stolen from.'

'This spot, it's just so perfect.'

'And safe.'

The soft addition drew her eyes to his face. 'I know I sound a bit over-protective at times but I promised Mum and Dad at the funeral that...' She felt her eyes fill and closed them, before pushing out a fierce, 'Sam is my responsibility and if I put him in harm's way I would never forgive myself.'

The image in his head of her, a younger, lonely figure by a graveside making a vow, had a heart-piercing poignancy. 'Such slender shoulders,' he said in a shiver-inducing undertone. 'To carry so much... You're both under my protection—you are safe. I'll keep the nightmares away.'

Tilda looked from his dark relentless eyes to the floating castle and didn't feel safe, but she did feel excited.

By the time she reached the villa she had run out of superlatives to describe it, though no doubt, had she asked, Sam could have helped out. When the infinity pool came into view, and the beach, being Sam he made time to assure his sister that swimming on a full stomach was not dangerous; it was an old wives' tale.

They pulled up on the forecourt where not only the pool was visible but the towering glass-paned extension that faced the sea.

'Wow, I take it that isn't part of the original building?' she said, unfastening her seat belt and sliding out, immediately hit by the pungent scent of lemon thyme that grew in the cracks between the terracotta paving.

Sam had run ahead and vanished round a corner.

'He'll be fine,' Ezio said, anticipating her anxiety.

'That is beautiful.' She stared at the glass extension, marvelling how it seemed to blend organically with the original stone. The arched roof and striking cupola were even more stunning close up than at a distance.

'The planners were quite sympathetic to a modern extension when they knew we were going to use traditional methods. The idea was not to replicate anything, just make something beautiful, and we employed local artisans. Of course, we borrowed a bit design wise. It is based roughly on a Victorian greenhouse, but we had modern techniques to draw on.'

'It reminds me of one at Kew!' she realised, spinning round to face him.

He nodded. 'We used similar materials—glass,

cast-iron and wood. The supporting arches inside are decorative steel. I'm glad you approve of my extension. My father thought I was insane.'

'Didn't he try and stop you?'

His expression hardened. 'He couldn't. My grandfather left Amphitrite to me. This was for him, to his memory—he was a great collector, and when it came to endangered plants and ferns he was an acknowledged expert.' He looked up at the building, then back to Tilda and smiled. 'Here, let me show you around. You might want to freshen up?'

Tilda raised a self-conscious hand to her hair and nodded. 'Should we find Sam first?'

'I'm sure he'll turn up. The poor kid's been cooped up all day. Let him— Of course, that's up to you.'

'It's so massive,' she said, casting an awed look up as they walked past a row of fountains to a massive, metal-banded double door.

'Big rooms, but actually not that many of them. No endless long corridors, and once you get the hang of the layout it's quite easy to navigate. The main living areas are mostly in, well, this white marble section, and the bedroom suites in the blue wing, a less grand local stone with no goddess connections. The kitchens and utility area are on the ground floor of the tower.' He nodded to the square gold tower. 'And my offices are on the top floor.'

'You must have quite a view from up there. An eagle in your eyrie.'

'Quite cruel of you to draw attention to my beak of a nose but, yes, it does have quite the view.'

Her glance automatically slid to the blade of a strong nose that bisected a face that was by any standards stunningly perfect.

'I'd call it more characterful.'

His grin flashed as he invited her to walk ahead of him.

Her first impression as she stepped inside was of space…and light. Light shone off every surface, the palette of soft French grey and white that picked out the stone friezes on the walls soothing. The elaborate mosaic in the floor was a pattern of concentric circles, again pale with splashes of sea-blue and gold.

'Large', he'd said, and he wasn't exaggerating. The massive square space's cavernous proportions were accentuated by a high-vaulted ceiling with dark, curved elaborately carved beams. It was sparsely furnished, even though you could have held a ball in the room. Most of the furniture, which was basically a few beautiful chairs and tables, was set around the wall, apart from a few large eclectic items set in the stone niches spaced around the room, and some modern paintings on the wall that provided dramatic splashes of colour.

Sitting centrally was a round stone table with a large stone urn from which spilled a fragrant and natural-looking display of flowers and foliage. She could imagine the low, modern chandelier set above dramatically highlighting it when it got dark.

'The friezes and the table were rescued from the original building—actually the pigsties.'

'Your home is very beautiful,' she murmured as she gazed around.

'It is your home for the moment.'

She smiled, knowing she would always feel like a guest.

'You look sad…'

She shook her head firmly. 'No, just a little overwhelmed.'

'Shall we save the tour until later? I'll take you to your rooms. This way.'

She followed him through one of the arches. This space was narrower and forked at the end. Along one wall, windows looked out onto a courtyard similar to the one they had entered through.

'So we take a right, and our suite is at the end.' He turned to the left fork. 'Sam's down there, and I had the sitting room turned into a study. I thought it would be more useful.'

Tilda had not heard the 'study' part… She had not got past the *'our'*.

'We are sharing a room? Over my dead body.'

'Dramatic,' he drawled. 'And, ultimately, a solution which really does not solve one hell of lot. I, however, have a much more practical idea…are you going to ask me what it is?'

She slung him a narrow-eyed look.

'I'll put a pillow between us, and I warn you, if you touch me I know self-defence.' His mockery

melted away, the expression in his dark eyes growing flat and hard. 'I said suite, not room—we have
rooms, two bedrooms, two dressing rooms and bath-
rooms and a large sitting room in between. I can
have locks put on if you fear that I will be overcome
by lust.'

By the time he was finished, her face was so hot it
could have lit up Athens. There was no face-saving,
or for that matter face-cooling, way to get out of this.

'Well, I feel pretty stupid now.'

She didn't look stupid, she looked like a crushed
flower at that moment. Young and a little lost.

'I'm starting think, Ezio, that you're a lot better
at this "keeping up appearances" thing than I am,'
she admitted ruefully. 'I hadn't thought what Sam
might think if we have rooms the opposite end of the
house.' She lifted her chin. 'You seem to have come
up with a very...workable solution.'

'You're not built for deception—you are too honest.'

Coming from Ezio, she wasn't sure if that was an
insult or a compliment, and his expression wasn't any
help. The tension shivering along his taut, golden
stubble-roughened jaw made her wonder if he wasn't
as uneasy at the prospect of the next six months as
she was.

Honest... He might think so, but Tilda couldn't
make the same claim, especially when she felt like
the big lie she was nursing was written across her
face in neon—namely that it was her too-handsome

boss who might need the lock on the door. Not *se-riously*, of course, because she would never get in-volved with a serial womaniser. She had more pride.

You married him, Tilda!

She had no idea why she stood rooted to the spot with the shock of it. It wasn't as if it was news. She had spent the last month counting the days off on the calendar and now it was here.

She had walked into this with her eyes wide open, and she was married, but not *involved*. God knew what the distinction was but it made her feel slightly less of a hypocrite.

Standing within the blast zone of his pure, *male* mind-numbing force field, she struggled to pull free of the sensual web that she had spun around herself.

Luckily, help was at hand, in the shape of a tall woman who wore her grey-streaked dark hair in a smooth pleat. Handsome rather than pretty, she wore a pair of wide-legged trousers and a pale-grey silk shirt. Tucked in behind her was Tilda's brother.

'I am so sorry I was not there to greet you,' she said, addressing her remark to them both. 'I have discovered this young man.'

Sam stepped forward reluctantly, and his wet hair told a story.

'Tilda, this is Sybil, the housekeeper here. Any problem, she is your go-to woman.'

Not for the sort of problems I have, Tilda thought, managing a forced smile.

'And, Syb, this is Tilda, my wife.' Now those were

two words he had never thought to hear himself say, but at least he could say them without flinching. Tilda could not hear them without doing just that.

Tilda assumed, as the other woman didn't stand there open-mouthed or go into shock, that she must have been given some warning about their married status.

The two women exchanged smiles and nods.

'We were about to send a search party out for you,' Tilda lied as she turned to her brother, brows raised. 'You decided on a dip, I see?' She didn't really mind. Sam was a strong swimmer, and actually she felt quite envious; she would give a lot to immerse her hot and sticky self into cool water. Swimming was the only sport she had ever been any good at, and she had passed on the skill her father had taught her to Sam.

'I was just giving you two some alone time,' Sam responded virtuously. 'And, in case you're worried, I didn't skinny dip. I left my pants on, which are a bit soggy now.'

'Syb, would you show Sam to his suite? We'll all catch up in the Fern House later.'

'Is that what you call it? Wow, Tilda, there is a cool—'

Ezio cut him off mid-flow. 'Later, Sam. She can see for herself.' He floated a comment in Greek to the housekeeper over Tilda's head and the other woman nodded before gesturing to Sam to follow her.

'This way, Sam.'

* * *

'Sam seems to have made himself at home.'

'A bit too much at home,' Tilda worried. It had never occurred to her that him liking life here too much would be an issue. 'It will be a wrench for him to leave.'

'You have barely arrived and the only thing you can talk about is leaving?'

Hearing the annoyance in his voice, she glanced up at the tall, sleek, beautiful male creature she was struggling to keep pace with and felt her throat close… He really was utterly gorgeous, even with his jaw clamped taut in annoyance.

'Well, I have to think ahead.'

He took a step ahead and turned to face her, slanting a glittering look at her face as he continued to walk backwards…

If I tried that, I'd fall flat on my face, she thought. She could simply not imagine Ezio doing anything that wasn't elegant and co-ordinated.

'Ever heard of living in the moment?'

'I did that once today…' The words were out before she could stop them and she was watching herself grab him and kiss him… That it had only happened today seemed impossible.

'And very nice it was too.'

His throaty murmur almost made her trip…before she sought a solution to the problem by removing her shoes. Hopping from one foot to the other with a lot of swear words was a useful distraction.

'I've got flats in my bag,' she grumbled. At some point, her bag had vanished…was it in the car?

Ezio stared at her small, narrow elegant feet, the toe nails painted pale-pink. He had never in his life considered a woman's feet a turn-on. 'I could carry you. Don't look at me like that. I have not just made an indecent suggestion.' His thoughts were a lot less pure, and, had she known where his tongue in his hot ever-developing fantasy that began at the arch of her foot had reached, she would have looked a lot more outraged. *Or not…?*

'I'm fine, thank you.'

He tipped his head, accepting her lie. 'It's not far now, and your luggage will be in our…sorry, *your*…room.'

They reached the room and he paused to let her enter before him. Tilda found herself in a pretty, light room. The open French doors faced a terrace with brightly coloured flowers set against the backdrop of the blue sea.

'The sitting room.' He made an expansive gesture that took in the room. 'Your room is that side. Mine…' He nodded to the second door. 'Nothing so scary as an inter-connecting bathroom. We are standing in the neutral zone… Oh, and you will find some clothes in the dressing room. The ones you rejected and a few others—and before you protest,' he inserted in a bored drawl that made her close her open mouth with a snap. 'These are not an indulgence but a necessity. In order to play a role convincingly, get into character, you need to dress the part. You are my wife.' The possessive note in this autocratic pronouncement should have made her laugh, but it didn't; instead, the quiver low in her belly became a thrum.

'And you think clothes are going to convince anyone of that?'

'I'm hoping your lingering look of love will seal the deal, *glikia mou.*'

'You are so up yourself!' she cried, her face flaming at his mockery.

'You'll miss me when I'm gone,' he teased, walking to the door and leaving behind the echo of his deep, throaty laughter.

The horrible possibility his mocking jibe was not a million miles from the truth was why she was resisting getting into the role…as much as she wanted to deny the attraction she was feeling. She wasn't blind to the real danger of buying into the fiction, getting so deep into character that she couldn't find the exit.

She needed to keep that exit in sight and not let Ezio spoil her for a man who one day might come along… Even if he didn't, she didn't want to spend her life comparing every man she met to this complex, infuriating man.

She walked into her bedroom which was complete with far too many mirrors, a stunning chandelier of wrought-iron and cut glass and, of course, the bed…a fairy-tale four-poster piled high with cushions.

Pre-warned, she still got a little shock when she opened the dressing-room door. The sheer volume of clothes hanging on the rails that lined the room took her breath away. She pulled open a couple of the drawers. She wouldn't have been human if the luxury fabrics, soft silks and delicate lace had not made her sigh with pleasure...and the thought of them against her skin.

The thought of someone peeling them away from her skin... Aware of the moist heat between her legs, she closed her eyes against the images, but they stayed there and there was no mistaking *whose* fingers she was imagining on her...

She needed to cool down; she needed a shower.

The bathroom was another jaw-dropper—double-ended beaten-copper bath tub, a view through the slatted shutters that was breath-taking and glass shelves lined with bottles of luscious-looking oils that invited her to take the tops off and inhale.

Tilda didn't, she headed towards the shower, which was the size of her bathroom at home, and stripped off, letting her clothes fall to the floor in a heap.

The controls looked as if they belonged in an alien space ship but, after pressing everything on the touch-pad control, something happened and water came at her from all sides.

She supposed it was adjustable but, rather than try to figure it out, she settled for having her skin pummelled clean by the jets. By the time she emerged, her skin was pink and glowing. Pity the same couldn't be said for her mind, which was still firing on all cylinders.

She was in the living room when there was a knock on the door. She was tightening the belt on one of the beautiful silk robes from the Aladdin's cave dressing room when the door opened.

The sense of anti-climax was intense.

Her brother walked in, looking clean and scrubbed. She recognised his expression with a sigh.

'So what do you want?'

'Me? Actually, I came to tell you dinner is ready when you are… The thing is, Tilda—you know, as this is your wedding night and all—I thought I might let you two…you know… You can do the whole candle thing and everything.'

'That's very considerate of you, Sam, but totally unnecessary.'

'I already asked Ezio.'

'And what did Ezio say?'

'That I had to ask you, but the thing is, there's this podcast I've been really looking forward to and this guy…a professor at… Well, you wouldn't know him, but he's really good. He makes astrophysics so *accessible*, you know what I mean? And a tray in my room would be good because I'm really exhausted and, quite honestly, if I have to watch you two *smouldering* at each other I'll throw up.'

'Sam, I… We… Oh, all right. But tomorrow,'

she warned sternly, 'You eat with us like a civilised human being.'

'Oh, God, yes…of course. Oh, thanks, Tilda—and it's just down the corridor, a sharp right and the other side of the hallway. The rooms kind of flow… Yeah,' he said, pleased with the description. 'They flow, so you just follow—follow the smell, I suppose.'

CHAPTER EIGHT

THIS WAS GETTING out of control, Tilda decided, standing back, hands on hips, to view the pile of clothes on the bed. Also, it was giving her a headache.

She shook her head—a mistake—and growled out an impatient, 'Get a grip, Tilda!'

For a split-second, she was tempted to dress for dinner in a pair of jeans and sweater, and not one of the selection of lovely cashmere ones beautifully folded on the shelves, but that might be a provocation too far. She didn't want to poke that particular tiger, which could get a bit unpredictable when roused.

No, definitely a gesture that could backfire, she decided, abandoning the idea with some regret.

But this indecisive dithering was slowly driving her crackers. She had never spent more than five minutes deciding what to wear…

Anyone would think she had someone to impress!

But then, she had never had so much choice, she thought, looking at the stack of designer garments piled high. How was she meant to know what a billionaire's wife would wear? Even a temporary one.

A small, secretive smile curved her mouth as she experienced a light-bulb moment. Yes, she knew the *perfect* way to make an impossible decision.

Eyes scrunched tight, she stepped towards the pile of dresses on the bed and burrowed her hand into the pile of silks and satins, letting her fingers close around a slithery piece of silk.

She opened them and held the dress up, a bias-cut calf-length in deep emerald-green. It was the sort of bold colour she rarely wore. The demure neck contrasted with the dramatic and daring low cowl-back that reached almost to her waist.

She had previously discarded it as being too bold, too not *her*... She shrugged and thought why not? She wasn't playing herself. The idea was oddly liberating.

She didn't want to fade into the background.

The idea of being looked at did not bother her so much...or was it the idea of being looked at by one particular person? It was hard not to feel confident when a man who looked like Ezio, a man who all women desired, looked at you the way he had... She gave a sinuous little shiver and felt scared and excited all at once. She felt like someone about to step out into the unknown.

Half an hour later, in a pair of spiky heels the like of which she had never owned in her life, she walked down the corridor, still feeling not quite like herself, but enjoying the swish of heavy silk against her legs as she walked, her heels tapping on the terracotta underfoot.

The breeze, scented with salt from the sea, wafted in through the open windows, the softness caressing the bare skin of her back and neck.

As she got to the end of the corridor, she glanced at her reflection in one of the windows to check her hair was still in place. A few soft, silky strands had escaped the loose chignon but otherwise it was still intact.

Sam had been right about the flow of the rooms in the living area. They did for the most part flow seamlessly on from one to another, giving the impression of space and light, each in its own individual way as beautiful as the one she had just left.

The light was fading now. A few lamps were on and several candles in the sconces had been lit, casting flickering patterns on the ceiling. She reached a massive living room, furnished, as the villa was throughout, with a combination of modern pieces and antiques. The vast sofas looked made for flopping in, but no one was.

The place was so quiet, she could hear a clock from the previous room ticking.

Ahead, she could see the formal dining room, but that too was empty. She sensed movement and turned her head, for the first time seeing that beyond the floor-length windows along one wall there was

another space, previously dark. She could now see
the golden reflection of light against the glass—the
famous Fern House, she assumed, as she walked to
a set of doors.

She was inside the fernery, the massive modern
glass house. The echo quotient went up as her heels
clicked on the floor. Tilting her head, she took in
the spot-lit carved wood and curved metal rafters
high above her head, the whole curved structure
appearing to be supported by four massive metal
pillars. The same scrolled carving was repeated in
the frames of the multi-paned wood and ornamental
steel-framed glass walls.

Uplighters set in the stone floor picked out artis-
tically placed groups of green foliage, and the raised
pond that filled the space with the trickle of water
took central position. Sofas were grouped at one end
around several low tables, and at the other end a dining table was laid, the candlelight leaving a glowing
nimbus of light around the pretty pots of flowers and
reflecting off the cut-crystal wine glasses.

The place seemed empty as she walked along the
side of the raised sunken pool, lights revealing the
fish swimming in lazy circles among the swaying
green fronds of aquatic plants.

'Good evening.'

For a brief, insane moment, she thought he had
materialised in front of her, but as sanity kicked
in she noted the open door and the breeze blowing
in that ruffled his dark hair. He carried the scent

of the warm evening air and green vegetation on his clothes.

As she watched him walk towards her, moving with the silent grace of a big, beautiful, sleek predator, her stomach started fibrillating.

She realised that she had just been standing there staring, and she didn't have a clue how long, and he was just a couple of feet from her.

'Hi!' she said brightly. 'I am… I'm late. Early…? Have I kept you waiting?'

'None of the above.'

He held out a hand that invited her to precede him. She tipped her head in acknowledgment and felt very glad that she had not come casual to make a point, not that she knew what that point would have been.

That's me…the rebel without a brain cell who is about to fall off her heels.

Ezio's only concession to casual was that he was not wearing a tie. His pale shirt was one of those she knew he had hand-made in Italy and ordered by the dozen; there were always a handful of un-opened ones in his office. He wore the shirt open at the neck, the open-button arrangement enough to reveal the strong column of his neck and deep olive-toned skin along with a tiny vee of skin at the base of his throat, suggesting that he was that glorious toasty colour all over.

Clean-shaven, there was no trace of the earlier stubble on his sculpted face. His suit was silver-grey, but it was the power not concealed by the supreme tailoring that made her shiver, not the perfect cut.

'Do I pass?'

She sucked in an embarrassed little gasp. 'I just thought, you changed… I didn't hear you…'

'I caught up on a few things. I keep some fresh things in my office. I didn't want to disturb you if you were resting.'

'Oh I see, like in London. Well, not the me resting part.'

'No, I have heard your boss is a bit of a taskmaster.'

She flung him a look. 'The you keeping things in your office part… I mean…' Her voice trailed off before she could sound any more like an inarticulate idiot.

This really didn't feel like London. In London there was no background accent of lush greenery. In London there had been an invisible professional barrier between them. Like those barriers down the motorway, it had provided safety…no collisions.

What would it feel like to collide with Ezio?

She lowered her eyes but she couldn't hide from the pulse at the apex of her thighs.

'The view from the shower here is better.' It was nothing on the view he had enjoyed from outside when he had turned his head and seen her standing there.

This was not a 'butterfly unfurling' moment or an 'ugly duckling into swan' transformation. In her dull office clothes, she had always been a beautiful woman, but standing there, gracefully poised on some crazy heels, the vivid green dress hugging her body and pulling tight against the thrust of her breasts and slender waist, she was bewitching, breathing-taking.

Mesmerised, he was rooted to the spot with white-hot lust. It took several dramatic inhalations to batter his instincts into submission before he could trust himself to approach her without wanting to sink to the floor with her—actually, he still did.

Tilda was involved in a very tough fight not to see him in the shower, but the carnal image of steamy water sliding off his water-slick skin flashed into her head, reducing her shaky inner calm to jelly.

She really had no idea what was happening to her… It was as if her hormones were having their revenge for being ignored for so long.

'None of the above.'

Panic floated briefly into her mind for the duration of the amnesia; she didn't have a clue what question he was responding to. Her breath snagged in relief as the memory surfaced above the sensual fog that had taken up residence in her head.

'I thought you might need to sleep. I hope it doesn't offend your sensibilities as much as it did the cook—please do not call her a chef; she will be insulted—but I wasn't sure what time we'd be eating, so I asked her to pre-prepare and leave things warming, which caused a minor meltdown. She considers heated trolleys an invention of the devil—or it might have been the seventies. I don't think she cares much for either.'

Smiling down at her, he pulled a chair out at the table. After a fraction of hesitation, she walked forward, making him think of a leggy, skittish colt likely to break for freedom at the last moment.

Her gliding grace was as natural as breathing, and all the more attractive because she remained utterly unaware that the way she moved made men watch her.

Standing behind her, he fought the impulse to tuck a behind her ear a stray strand of hair that floated across her cheek. At least he was free to enjoy the scent of her shampoo and take in all the details of the lovely length of her neck, the delicate protrusion of her shoulder blades and the line of her spine. A ballet dancer would have been jealous of the supple strength in the fine network of muscles under the silky skin of her back.

'She offered to stay.'

'Your cook?' Tilda said, faintly trying to jolt her brain into active life, but at least able to breathe now he wasn't standing so close. She watched through her lashes as he pulled out a seat opposite her but didn't immediately sit down.

'She has her grandson visiting her. He's an undergraduate at Oxford and she doesn't get to see him that much.'

'Oh, no, that's fine…that's very considerate of you.'

He pushed away the stab of guilt. His motives had been far from altruistic; he had just seized on the excuse to have dinner with Tilda with no interruptions.

He was playing with fire and he knew it, but it didn't seem to matter. A kind of madness had taken hold when he had seen her standing there, and he wasn't fighting it very hard. He wasn't fighting, he was going with the flow, and it felt...dangerous... but danger always had attracted him.

Some inner sense told her that if she didn't break the spell now she never would. 'I should look in on Sam...' she said, half-rising. 'I wasn't sure where his room was.'

'I already have looked in.' On one of the several occasions he had stood outside their suite door, debating whether to go inside.

'Oh!' She sank back down, thinking, *at least I tried...though not so desperately hard.*

'He is stuffing his face again and talking astrophysics.'

'And how goes the hunt for a new PA? Have you considered Rowena?'

'The office again!' He sighed. 'History repeating itself...'

Tilda gave a mystified shake of her head. 'Sorry I don't...?'

'*Angela* persuaded me to give *you* a chance.'

Tilda smiled. 'Did she? I never knew. I wonder how she is.' Tilda really regretted losing contact with the older woman. 'It's tragic...she was only thirty-one.' On the last occasion they'd met, Angela had been coping with the hair loss from chemo with typical Angela humour.

'And now she is thirty-five, and she and her husband have started a business and have adopted their first child.'

Her eyes flew wide. 'She had the all-clear!' Her delight morphed into astonishment. '*You* kept in touch!'

'She worked for me for eight years—I am their child's godfather.' Probably not a very good one, but he had been touched to be asked, and little Arthur was probably the closest he'd ever come to parenthood. Actually, he thought, self-correcting his thought, there was no probably about it.

He remembered his godson's birthday, sent him Christmas gifts and had set up a trust fund for his education, but he didn't *know* the child; he felt no *emotional* connection—certainly not the sort that he felt for Sam. In a few short weeks the teen had made a big impression and Ezio liked to think he had actually been of some help to the kid too.

'Well, send her my love the next time you speak to her. So, does your housekeeper live in…and other staff…?' She had seen a group of men looking busy in the garden.

'Sybil has a cottage in the grounds and the head gardener, Nikos, lives in the gatehouse. A contractor comes in for the heavy-duty stuff these days, but he has a few men who help, and a youngster he is training up to replace him.'

'The garden here looks very beautiful,' she said, relieved to be talking about something normal. 'I can't wait to explore.'

'They are actually more upkeep than the house. Sybil makes do with a couple of locals who come in daily, and more as needed, but the place is empty a lot of the year.'

Processing this information in her head, Tilda came up with the information she had been fishing for in a roundabout way—the place was empty except for Sam, who would probably fall asleep over his computer screen.

'Wine?'

'Oh God, yes please,' she said with feeling. Then, catching the quiver of his lips, she added quickly, 'I'm quite thirsty.' Her eyes went to the water jug and she grabbed it and filled her glass, looking at him over the rim as she raised it to her lips.

'And you missed out on the champagne on the flight.'

'It's been a long day.'

Her heart hammering like a drum, Tilda watched him fill her wine glass. The tension in the air was so dense it had an almost audible static buzz…or was that in her head?

'This really is very beautiful.' She tipped her head back to look at the gracefully arched beams. 'The craftsmanship is very special.'

He retook his seat and raised his own glass.

The stem felt slippery when she picked up hers, then she realised it was her hands, not the glass.

'To us.'

She lifted her drink, steaming the glass with her breath as she held it there, looking at him over the rim, fighting the impulse to say there was no *us*.

'To our first dinner together.'

'It isn't.'

'What?'

'It's not our first dinner together. I flew up to Edinburgh that time because you'd forgotten those papers and your date had stood you up. You had booked at that posh French place and you took me, then she rang and said... Well, I don't know what she said, but it was obviously a pretty good offer, because you were out of there like greased lightning.'

A comical expression of dismay spread across his face. 'Oh God, I'd forgotten.'

'Oh, don't worry, you paid the bill before you left, and left money for my taxi, and I drank the whole bottle of that very expensive wine; it was actually really good.' Only just realising as she relayed the details that the memory still stung, she took a gulp of her wine. This was probably good too, but the truth was she was no judge.

He sat there looking stunned. He had blanked the occasion, and the memory of reacting to that phone call as if it was a lifeline, because it had rung at the same moment that he had acknowledged that taking his PA out of the office had been a mistake. He'd been *noticing* too much—her laugh, which was full-blooded and throaty, which he had never heard in the office. That her skin in the candlelight had looked quite astonishingly smooth.

'Shall I help myself?' she said, getting up and approaching the trolley. 'Wow, you should be very nice to your…cook. She is good,' she said, inhaling the scent of lamb in the rich, fragrant sauce.

She retook her seat with the plate and smiled across at him. 'You're not eating.'

'I was a selfish bastard,' he said, his voice harsh with self-recrimination.

She set her elbows on the table and looked at him. 'You won't get any arguments from me.'

'I don't remember her name…' he said, half to himself.

'Well, mine is down on a certificate, so that will make it easier.'

His frown deepened. 'Do not compare yourself. You're nothing like…' His dark eyes settled on her face. 'No man could forget you.'

She put her fork down, struggling to feign an appetite the tension had sucked away, her stomach churning with a strange mix of emotions. It felt raw… she felt raw… She felt suddenly incredibly angry.

'I did feel ridiculous, sitting there, but I mostly felt ridiculous because I'd been excited. That was the most expensive restaurant I'd ever been to, and when you left the snooty waiter looked down his nose at me all evening, and I didn't call him on it—I didn't even say a word—and when I left, no actually I did, I said *thank you*… Can you believe it?' She came to a breathless halt, a look of horror spreading across her face. 'I have no idea where that came from. It was ages ago and—'

'Tilda, I am truly sorry.' He leaned forward towards her, the image of her sitting there alone driving a stake through his heart.

'Oh, I believe you mean it now, just like you probably mean it when you say *I love you* to the women in your bed, but—'

'No, I don't.'

'Don't what?'

'I don't say I love you. I've never said…'

She watched his expression change but, before she could interpret the look on his face, he veiled his eyes and leaned back in his seat.

'You never…?'

'I said it once…it was a long time ago. It's the sort of thing you say when you propose.'

'You were engaged?' She didn't laugh but she came close.

'No, she actually rejected me.' His lips twisted in a self-derisory half-smile as he recalled the events.

By the time he been brought to the point where he had declared his eternal and undying love in quite a dramatic way, as he recalled, Lucilla could finally afford to be honest about her feelings. She had by that point passed on the information she had been milking him for to the lover he later discovered she had left her husband for. The same husband whose supposed cruelty had filled him with vengeful fury. It was easy to see now why she had been so alarmed when he had announced his intention to confront the guy.

The memory of his younger in-love self, confiding all his hopes and dreams for a future he planned to share with her, made his gut tighten in self-contempt. For a long time afterwards, he'd tortured himself with the thought of her laughing with her lover over his sentimental drivel.

His big romance had been revealed as industrial espionage taken to an extra level. When Lucilla had not been not in his bed, she'd been in bed with one of the main rivals of the firm started by his grandfather and continued by his father—the firm that had been absorbed into Angelos Inc, but even then it had been worth three months seducing the boss's son.

'Don't get me wrong, I had fun. Not just the lovely information you gave me, I had permission to enjoy your youth and...enthusiasm... It has been an exhausting six months for me. I was actually prepared to put up with your sentimental rubbish and poetry for the sex.'

No matter how the memory made him feel, he wanted to remember, so that if he ever felt the urge to mistake sex for anything deeper it would be there to pull him back from the brink of making a fool of himself.

He had not needed the memory; he had not felt that way about any woman since. If the experience had killed off that part of him, he was glad of it.

He had learnt that day how to protect what was his—like chess, his father had said when he had confessed what he had done, you sacrifice your pawn to ensure you win... Play the long game.

His father had made his sacrifice and it had turned out to be Ezio himself.

The only way he'd learn from his mistakes, his father had told him, was if he wasn't there to clean up the mess. He'd had his chance and he'd blown it, he'd been told, and life didn't offer second chances. Or, his father didn't.

Tilda directed her gaze at her food but found her eyes tugged back to his face; his shuttered expression was hard to read.

'You were heartbroken, I suppose,' she tossed at him, stirring the food as she regarded him through her lashes, still waiting for the cynical punchline.

'Badly bruised, but I recovered,' he assured her, wondering what had possessed him to share this unnecessary information with her.

The half-smile faded and her lips flattened. It was this down-playing that made her realise that this wasn't a joke. 'You really... Oh, God!' She gulped remorsefully. 'I am so sorry, I didn't mean to...'

He gave a hard laugh, amazed that anyone could leak empathy this way. 'Open old wounds? You didn't,' he assured her. They were open because he had kept them that way, as a reminder. 'Anyway, I had my revenge.'

'What was that?'

'I got very rich, she let all that lovely money slip through her fingers and it was lovely money she was after.'

No one who had got over it, as he'd claimed, could sound that bitter. Who was the woman who had broken through the cynical shell of Ezio Angelos? And was the animosity a cover for the fact he still loved her?

Well aware of the danger of allowing her imagination full rein, she closed down the line of speculation but struggled not to feel empathy. The focus of her antagonism was for the faceless woman, until the irony of what she was doing hit her—yesterday she would have sworn that Ezio didn't have a heart to break and now, well, she was aching for him.

And she had to admit he didn't look much like a classic *victim;* actually, not any sort of victim. Conscious of pain, she glanced down where her hands lay on her lap clenched into white-knuckled fists. Flexing her fingers, she saw the deep red half-moons cut into her palm.

Tilda's tender heart ached. The idea that out there existed a woman who he had never recovered from left her feeling angry. The nameless woman had made him feel he had to guard his heart, had made him lock himself off from love.

Tilda didn't realise she'd physically shaken her

head to clear the anger until she saw him looking at her, his head tilted questioningly to one side. She pushed away her plate, all appetite gone.

'So, were you together a long time?' she asked, casually wondering if the other woman had ever drunk from the glass she was holding... She put it down abruptly.

'No.'

Her lips tightened at the clipped response. She felt frustration well up inside her. His tight-jawed expression made it crystal clear she could fish as much as she liked but he was not opening up any more.

'You can sulk as much as you like, Tilda... Do *you* want to talk about previous lovers?'

'I am not sulking and I don't have...' She stopped dead and watched the expressions move like some sort of slide show across his face before settling into stunned disbelief.

She sat there folding her napkin with geometric precision before getting to her feet. 'I think actually I might... It's been a long day.'

'Are you saying you have never had a...? That you're a...?' He shook his head; even *saying* it sounded ridiculous.

'I'd say that's none of your business.' At least for once she was looking down on him, and boy, did she need all the advantage she could get.

'And I thought *I* had problems.'

'I don't have a problem—well, except you. I made a choice some time ago that I wasn't going to expose

Sam to a stream of uncles…and one-night stands are not my style.'

'Don't knock it till you've tried it,' he drawled. 'So weren't you worried when we got married that I might want to take it to the next level?'

'You mean sex? I'm a virgin… I can say the word, I don't have hang-ups…and I was not worried, because if that was what you wanted I feel sure you'd have included how many times and in what positions in the small print; you covered everything else!' she accused with breathless disdain.

His sloe-dark eyes glittered as he watched her lose it big time, the passion spilling from her… He watched the movement of her small breasts under the silk, making him think of them filling his hand—the perfect size. His heart rate slowed in time with the blood pouring in his throbbing temples and points south as he visualised those perfect breasts pushing up into him, her arms around him.

'No hang-ups,' he purred. 'No fun.'

'It depends on what you consider fun, and while we're being frank—' Some grain of sense slipped through the fog of fury in her head and she stopped dead.

'By all means.' His lean body rigid, he gestured for her to continue, and languidly crossed one ankle across the other as he pushed the chair back from the table with a loud scraping sound.

'Your bed-hopping strikes me as pathetic,' she

flung at him. 'It makes me shudder just to imagine anything so…so…empty.'

'Your prissy, judgmental, little virgin nose is quivering.'

'And, for the record, no, I wasn't even slightly worried because that…*sex*…would be *my* decision, not yours.'

His narrowed eyes gleamed and he smiled, looking lean and dangerous as he shook his head in reproach and murmured, 'Always polite to wait until you're asked, *glikia mou*.'

CHAPTER NINE

SHE STOOD THERE, fists clenched, and shook her head, her body trembling with anger. 'You are the most totally horrible man I have ever encountered!'

And once more with feeling, Tilda mocked the voice in her head. Nothing she said could make even the slightest impression on Ezio.

'What's the point?' she asked, throwing up her arms in an attitude of defeat as she delivered a final dirty look before swivelling away sharply on her heels, the action causing the fabric of her dress to flare, tighten then flare again around her legs as she began to stalk away.

Ezio knew that the image of her retreating bottom outlined by silk would would stay with him… The heaviness in his groin was not going to vanish any time soon either.

'Horrible…?'

Her teeth clenched as his mocking voice followed her. 'Can't you do better than that?'

'You are…' She twisted back and found he was

no longer sitting down but standing, looking big, dangerous and beautiful, about six inches from her. The shock made her sway slightly.

His hands landed on her shoulders. The weight provided an anchor, the slow, sensual movement of his thumbs across her collar bones making it hard to keep her eyes open. Her neck felt too weak to support her head.

'I am totally desperate.' He moved one hand to her chin, bringing her face up to his so she could see the tension drawn into the planes and hollows of it. She could see the dark fire burning in his eyes. 'I'm asking, *glikia mou*, so what's your answer? Shall we add an amendment to that contract?'

Her lashes fluttered and she looked up at him. Need *ached* through her like a fever.

Feed a fever—wasn't that what they said? Tilda was pretty sure it was actually *starve* a fever, but she decided the situation warranted a little poetic licence.

'You're asking?' Her husky response was barely above a whisper. Her throat felt aching and tight.

'I am.' At this point he was so desperate beyond reason to shape her softness into him and sink into her, taste every delicious inch of her body, that he would have *begged* if necessary. The fact she was a virgin should have automatically put her off-limits. It was a responsibility that he should run from…or should at least have had had a 'cold shower' effect… but he was beyond cooling, beyond sense.

Tilda was shaking all over now, so hard her teeth

were juddering as if she were someone with a fever; she was burning up from the inside out.

Like someone in a dream, she stretched up and took his face between her hands, her fingers cool against his warm skin. The warning voice in the back of her head was now the faintest whisper.

'My answer is yes please,' she whispered, staring upwards to his mouth, his really sinfully beautiful mouth.

Sin had never looked so good to Tilda.

He stood, body rigid. Fine tremors, like those of a racehorse held back at the starting gates, were running through his body as she moved her soft lips across his. He stood still while her tongue slid tentatively and then with more confidence into his mouth, and then his control broke.

A low growl vibrated in his throat and he took charge of the kiss, plundering the warm, secret recesses of her mouth with a ravenous, primal hunger that shocked and excited her more than anything she had ever known. Then when she was faint and breathless the hunger slowly transitioned to a slow dance of seduction, of strokes and probing, retreat and advance, until nothing existed in her world but the taste of him. All she could smell was him and all she could feel was the ache inside her.

When the kiss stopped she was plastered up against him like a second skin, her breath coming in a series of frantic, uneven gasps.

Fire flamed in his eyes as he wrapped his arms

around her middle, picking her up so that their faces were level. Thrilled to the core by the display of casual masculine strength, she wound her arms around his neck, sliding her fingers deep in his abundant hair as she kissed the side of his mouth, then ran her tongue experimentally around the inner aspect of his lower lip. He jerked her back a little and, holding her gaze, slowly let her slide down his body, allowing her to feel his erection as the hardness pressed into softness of her belly the whole way.

Once on her feet, he pushed her a little way from him before he held out a hand.

'Come.'

She stared up at him, utterly mesmerised. Standing there feet apart, his face a golden mask of need, he presented a pagan image, wild and unrestrained, that imprinted itself on her retinas as she reached for him.

Walking backwards, his eyes not leaving her face for a moment, he led her to a large, low couch before drawing her to him and kissing her while his big, capable hands and clever fingers moved in slow sweeps over her body, caressing her curves through the silk and bare skin he discovered on her back, awakening every nerve cell in her body into tingling painful life.

Little soft, mewling sounds left her mouth and were lost in his as he kissed his way up the curve of her exposed neck. Her back arched as he lowered her onto the wide sofa, sweeping the cushions off in one movement. He removed her crazy heels one by one, throwing each shoe over his shoulder.

She watched, her lids half-lowered, as he rested one knee on the sofa and, bracing the opposite foot, he took hold of one of her feet. She let out a slow gasp of surprise as he ran his finger down the high arch of it before licking the places his finger had touched.

The other foot received the same treatment, and then his fingers and tongue moved higher, sliding under the silk of her dress, reducing her in a matter of seconds to a mass of inarticulate craving.

'I think,' he said hoarsely. 'We can dispose of this.' He took the hem of her dress, scrunching the fabric in his hands as he worked his way up. She gave a little wriggle, lifting her hips to let the silk slide up and over her bottom, and then after a couple of expert tugs it joined her shoes.

Then his fingers went to the back of her head and, finding the clip that secured the loose knot, he freed her hair, watching with an expression of satisfaction as it fell in a silky skein down her back.

'I've been wanting to do that since you walked in... I've been wanting to do a lot of things.'

'Such as?' she murmured huskily, feeling bold and womanly, feeling the power of her sex for the first time in her life.

He smiled his slow 'devil on steroids' smile that made her insides shake. 'You're in a such a hurry.'

He was not wrong; she was consumed by an urgency to have to have it all right now.

Wearing the satin camisole and a pair of silk shorts, the only thing the cut of the green dress had allowed, she fought the urge to hide behind her hands, instead letting them lie clenched at her sides, suddenly painfully conscious that she was not what he was used to.

He just sat there on the edge of the sofa looking down at her, his eyes watching the rise and fall of her breasts against the thin satin covering, the thrust of her nipples pushing through the fabric.

'You're beautiful,' he groaned, bending forward to cover the hard nubs with his mouth through the fabric. Her body arched again and she sighed at the exquisite burning pleasure of the contact, which left wet marks against the silk.

He raised himself to take up where he'd left off on her legs, stroking her foot as he continued his carnal journey along the inner aspect of first one thigh and then the other. By the time he reached the burning wet apex of her legs, she was making hoarse little wild sounds.

He took a few moments to shrug off his jacket and then fight his way out of his shirt.

One hand trailing limply on the floor, Tilda watched him, catching her breath as his bronzed torso was revealed. She squirmed, the kick of lust low in her belly and the insistent pulse between her legs making her moan.

The sound brought his eyes to her face as he unfastened his belt and unzipped his trousers then, holding her eyes with a heavy-lidded, carnal stare, he kicked them aside before freeing his erection from his underwear then it too was slid down his long, lightly hair-roughened legs.

Tilda could barely breathe. The emotional constriction in her throat reduced her breathing to a series of shallow gasps. He was the epitome of everything male. There was not an ounce of spare flesh on his lean body to conceal the perfect musculature of his body, the strength of his shoulders, the muscular slabs across his flat belly.

'Now you, I think.'

An expression of purpose stamped on his lean face, he applied himself, first to her camisole, which was disposed of in one slick motion. He paused then for a moment, staring with a mixture of stark greed and reverence at her hard-tipped breasts, purring out a low, stomach-shuddering, '*Perfect*,' before removing her seriously damp shorts.

She was quivering as he then arranged his long length beside her and, with one hand between her legs, he pulled her up against him hard, his hand between them as he focused his carnal campaign on the wet aching folds between her legs.

The first skin-to-skin contact drew a shocked long, low moan from her parted lips and she pushed her small breasts against the solidity of his warm chest. Then, as his clever fingers slid over her slickness, teasing the delicate folds and tight, aching nub, she lost all sense of self. There was just the pleasure and the ache.

When the rhythm stopped, she let out a small cry of protest but was quickly distracted. Ezio was kissing and licking his way down her body, drawing keening moans of pleasure as he left a tingling trail that went deeper than the surface, it went to her very core.

Her heavy-lidded eyes opened; his body was curved over her.

'Oh my God, you are so perfect...' she breathed, placing her palms against his chest, spreading her fingers, feeling the thud of his heart, the satiny texture of his skin.

His face was all sharp, fierce angles, the sybaritic line of his cheekbones drawn knife-sharp by the bands of colour scoring the crests. Her fingertips slid with growing confidence over the hard slabs of his stomach before she slid lower, pausing for a moment in her carnal exploration as he sucked in a sharp breath, her tongue caught between her teeth.

Then she reached the hard column of his erection and tightened her fingers, feeling the throb of his silky-smooth shaft.

'Later...not now... Now I need to be inside you, Tilda,' he rasped. 'I need to have you tight around me.'

Kneeling over her, her face between his big hands, he rained kisses on every inch of her skin before he finally claimed her mouth. As he kissed her with a wild passion she equally matched, she felt as though he'd drain her.

Resting on his elbows, he lowered himself slowly and teasingly, first against her belly and then the mound of her sex, making her back arch. Only his hands on the crest of her hips kept her grounded.

His powerful chest was heaving, as though he was fighting against some invisible barrier to draw in air, the barely repressed raw wildness in his face exciting her more than she would have thought possible. The danger in him was an aphrodisiac, yet his touch as he ran a thumb down her cheek was so gentle, tender, a sharp contrast to the passion.

Fighting the urge to take her right here, right now, he battled to contain the madness that was consuming him. Those little throaty sounds coming from her parted lips, and the wanton glow in her green eyes, were sense- and self-sapping.

This was a kind of madness he had never experienced before.

Still kissing, he reached for the trousers that lay in a heap on the floor beside the sofa, pausing only to swear when his fingers did not immediately locate the foil package in the pocket, and grunting when he did.

She'd have begged him to take her, but her vocal cords wouldn't work; she was just a mass of craving, screaming nerve endings. But it was OK; she didn't need to beg or plead.

There was no pain, just a blissful sense of relief as her body expanded and adapted to accommodate him.

He sank into her, slow and careful, feeling the pulsing of her tight body around him, aware that this was all new to her. He always satisfied his lovers—it was matter of pride for him, and he gained pleasure from their enjoyment—but this was different.

This wanting to make it good for her was more… The emotion that he had excised with surgical precision from the sex act was back…not that this complication mattered to him in the slightest at that moment. All that mattered was Tilda, her heat, the rightness of being inside her.

Her head tucked into his shoulder, where he breathed words of encouragement, and other words which she couldn't translate but still excited her. Clutching his sweat-slicked back, she met his thrusts, sinking into herself with him until nothing existed as the pressure built inside her.

She felt aware of every individual nerve ending, floating feet above the ground at the same time, then as her muscles clenched around him she found herself striving for something just out of her reach, encouraged by the throaty, raw and often indecent coaxing in her ear.

Then she was falling, flickering lights behind her eyelids as nerve endings fired, the heat bathing every contracting muscle in her body as she felt him thrust into her one last time before he collapsed on top of her.

She enjoyed his weight for a few moments before he rolled off her. Wedged in the narrow space between him and the back of the sofa, she turned onto her side and curled against his body.

After a moment he started to stroke her hair. She sighed and kissed the damp skin of his chest. 'What are you thinking about?' she asked when their breathing patterns had slowed.

Ezio was avoiding thinking; if ever there was a moment for living in the moment, this was it.

'I am thinking that we should do that properly in a bed.'

'I think I like improper,' she said, her cheeks heating at her own audacity.

'*Theos*, I was definitely getting that impression too, *yineka mou*. Let us go and explore the improper possibilities a bed offers.'

CHAPTER TEN

'RELAX, HE'LL BE FINE,' Ezio said, placing his hand on the small of Tilda's back. He had adapted his stride to her heels and the disparity between their inside leg measurements as they walked towards the car. 'And don't look back.'

She flashed him a look. The last time he had said 'relax' had been earlier that morning, when he had revealed that they were having lunch in Athens at a world-renowned restaurant as the guest of Saul and his wife.

He had chosen his moment pretty well. Tilda had been quite mellow, having woken up to a naked man who, it turned out, *was* the sex god the tabloids called him, looking as though he wanted to eat her.

The next reveal had been made after he had doubled down on the 'sex god' thing and stopped her detaching herself from the post-coital warmth of his body, reminding her that Sam's induction day didn't start until eleven-thirty.

She hadn't needed that much persuading.

'There might be a few others at lunch...' He had dropped this additional information while stroking her back.

The rest of the information had had been extracted slowly, and when Tilda had the full picture of what her day would entail she had leapt out of bed. The full guest list for the *casual little* lunch party made it obvious that that it would be neither casual nor little.

Sitting at the table with them would be a UK government minister and his wife, a well-known journalist and his husband and a couple of highly placed Greek officials, and she assumed their partners, along with the inventor of an eco-fuel and, last but not least, an actor-director of award-winning films. His equally successful beautiful wife was away shooting on location.

'How could you do this to me?' She didn't wait for a response; she'd had plenty of time to get ready for a meeting with a headmaster, but now this... Now she had to find an outfit that was acceptable for *both* occasions. She had finally settled on understated. She glanced down, experiencing a quiver of uncertainty at her choice.

The shift she was wearing was a smoky-grey silk mixture, high at the neck with a high waistline, tiny pleats stopping it from being figure-hugging.

The fabric was butter-soft and it was classic, short but not indecently so; she could live with the amount of leg it revealed.

Navy rather than silver, and soft suede rather than

leather, the heels she wore today were similar in style to the ones that Ezio had removed last night… The memory sent a rush of warmth through her body and stoked the phantom feeling low in her belly. It was as if, even though he wasn't inside her, her body was reluctant to let go of the feeling.

Her thoughts drifted… If she'd had an ounce of sense, she wouldn't have let it happen. She knew she was heading for massive hurt; the measure of her madness was she'd make the same choice again— she'd take that reckless step into the unknown.

There had been moments during the morning when she'd felt as though she were still falling and a sense of unreality would hit her, almost as if she were living someone else's life.

She felt lighter, somehow, as if the responsibilities that had been resting on her shoulders had lifted. She knew it was only temporary but she was going to enjoy it while it lasted… She was going to enjoy Ezio and explore this hitherto unexpected sensual side of her personality that he had revealed.

She hardly recognised the person she was becoming, the things she was feeling. It was if some invisible protective film had been peeled away from her skin… The image of long, brown fingers peeling layers of clothing off her skin that appeared in tandem with the thought sent a surge of heat through her body.

A moment later, the heat was surging again!

'You look very beautiful.'

'God, you make me sound like a trophy wife!'

His brows lifted at her spiky response. 'You and those compliments…why do you deflect them? And *trophy*? You are no one's trophy. You are your own woman.'

Blinking at the compliment, she wondered, did she really *deflect* them?

She was her own woman, but surrendering to him and her own sensuality had given her another sense of power. Who would have thought that surrender could be so liberating?

Once inside the car, it purred to life.

'Is it far?'

'No, not far.'

'Do you think that he, Saul, is he testing…?'

'I think this is lunch.'

She flashed a look of irritation at his perfect profile. 'I don't see how you are so calm. This matters to you—it matters enough to marry me!'

'Relax or people will think we have just had a lover's tiff.'

'Is that why you slept with me, to make things look more realistic?'

She knew she'd made him angry, but she couldn't bring herself to apologise. After all, it was a legitimate question, it wasn't as if he lacked anything in the ruthlessness department.

'You think I manipulated you into my bed?'

She shook her head and lifted her chin. 'No, you didn't take me anywhere I didn't want to go.' She sensed some of the tension in his powerful shoulders slacken.

'You took me some places too.' *Life-changing places,* said the voice in his head, which he determinedly ignored. 'Don't over-think this. We are enjoying quite spectacular sex for six months. I don't see a bad side, do you?' he said, the comments meant for himself as much as her. His eyes swivelled sideways for a split second before he added, almost against his will, 'I slept with you because I couldn't *not* sleep with you. I hate these social things too—just be yourself at lunch.'

'Have you known Saul long?'

It was hard to make ordinary conversation with Ezio words *couldn't not* playing on a loop in her head.

'In a way. Years ago, I applied for a job with him. Let's just say that my background did not do me any favours. He started with nothing, and he's justly proud of the fact—and also fond of reminding people of the fact. He sent me packing.'

'So taking his company is your way of payback?'

'Is that what you think?' He shrugged and then thought, why shouldn't she think that? 'There is no *taking* involved.' He was paying a good price, or he would be, if Saul could move past his ancient feud with George Baros. Did either of them remember what had started it? Probably, and they had spent the years since polishing their enmity. 'I do not allow emotion to get in the way of good business. Revenge is the flipside of sentimentality; I don't allow either to cloud my judgement…unlike Saul.but I understand his suspicions.'

'But you said he was paranoid.'

'He is, but as they say, just because you are paranoid does not mean there is no conspiracy. A man who trusts too easily is a fool.'

'Do you ever trust anyone? Sorry, I didn't mean…'

'No offence taken. I don't even trust my own instinct sometimes.'

The plan had seemed so safe—*she* had seemed so safe—and now the goal posts had been shifted. Outside the office, his PA was something very different, and without warning. In his bed, she was all his dreams and fantasies made real.

If he hurt her, he'd hate himself…but would it stop him hurting her? Ezio knew himself well enough to doubt it. Tilda aroused his dormant protective instincts, but the irony was, the only thing she needed protecting from was him.

'Why were you looking for a job?' she asked, puzzled.

'My father does not do second chances. He kicked me out, so between them Saul and my father are responsible for my success. They wouldn't give me a job, so I made my own. I started my own company and in four years was in a position to buy out the family firm.'

He down-played the achievement but Tilda, who

knew all about his meteoric rise, knew better. 'Your father sounds...'

'Oh, he is worse, much worse!' Ezio's laughter held no humour. 'He made my mother's life a misery, and as they say the apple doesn't fall too far from the tree.'

He could tell from her expression that she had heard the warning. He owed her that much; he didn't want her thinking that he was something he wasn't.

He felt a sudden wild urge of longing for his life as it had been—ordered, calm and he not responsible for anyone but himself... He felt protective of her now; he felt... He wouldn't even let himself think the word buried deep in his heart. He would always revert to type; he knew this.

'You're dying to ask what I did that was so bad to make my father sack me, aren't you?'

'No!' she lied.

'I fell in love.' The cynicism in his voice was bitter enough to sour sugar. 'It turned out the love of my life was only interested in pillow talk. She passed on the secrets I spilled to a rival company. I was a ridiculous young fool.'

'She was the one you...?'

'Yes, I proposed to.' *You started this, Ezio, so there's no point moaning that she has run with it.* He was going to have to rein in this impulse to open up to her.

One sentence, but it explained so much. Her emotions high, she felt her eyes fill with tears. 'Oh, God, that's…'

'A learning experience that has stood me in good stead.'

Tilda didn't know which one she hated most—the father who'd discarded his son, or the woman who had used him. Both had made him the man he was today… Because of his trust issues, he had built a ten-feet wall around his emotions.

'I feel sorry for Saul.' Maybe because he could be Saul in thirty years' time. 'None of his children have any interest in the legacy…which of course plays in my favour; if they did, there is no way he'd be selling. This is his way of making sure that what he created carries on and he can still be a part of it.'

His bleak outlook brought a frown to her brow. 'But your children might not feel that way…'

'A father—*me*…?' His rich laughter had a hard edge. 'Can you *really* see that, Tilda?'

She could, and the image in her head of Ezio playing with a dark-haired baby broke her heart. She nursed the secret hurt to herself and said with quiet sincerity, 'You've been good for Sam, you've helped him a lot. I think you'd make a good father.'

The restaurant was not large, and outside there was nothing to suggest it was anything special except for the upmarket cars in the car park. Inside it was all exposed brick and industrial furniture, with some probably very expensive modern art on the walls.

All the tables were full. Tilda did not feel over-dressed—though perhaps under-jewelled. They were met by the *maître d'*, who obviously knew Ezio. As they walked through, conversation stopped and heads turned, eyes following the progress of the tall, dynamic figure she walked beside. It was a bizarre experience for Tilda, but she supposed a normal day at the office, or on this occasion out-side it, for Ezio.

They were led outdoors where there was a se-ries of intimate courtyards, clearly much coveted by A-listers. Saul, it seemed, had commandeered an entire courtyard for the lunch party.

The *maître d'* left them at the ivy-covered arch that led into their courtyard and gestured with a smile, adding, 'You are the last to arrive.'

'Oh, God… I feel sick.'

'You're hyper-ventilating.'

'No, I'm taking deep, calming breaths.' *Just too many and too fast.* She squared her shoulders and tried not to think of Ezio being a perfect father. 'I'll be fine.'

He laid his hands on her shoulders. 'You don't look fine. You look like you have something uncom-fortable shoved up—'

'Ezio!'

His grin appeared. 'Better, but you still don't look like a woman on her honeymoon.' He bent his head and kissed her long and hard. As he drew back, she felt the hair she had spent an age arranging in a really sleek knot tumble free.

Her mouth opened in a silent 'O' of shock.

'Now, that is *definitely* better. If I had a table here right now to bend you over…!'

He gave her a gentle push towards the table, just at the same time as she promised Ezio, in a voice that upheld her drama teacher's opinion that she had excellent projection, that she would kill him.

Hair spilling down her back, she saw the faces at the table looking their way, and her sense of humour kicked in; she started to laugh.

Ezio smiled as soon as he heard the contagious deep, throaty sound. He knew she had the room in the palm of her little hand… He thought about being in the palm of her hand himself and it took him a few moments to follow her to the table.

Their host stood behind her chair and Tilda spoke to the entire table. 'Sorry about that. I spent hours on my hair and…' She nodded to Ezio.

'I prefer it loose,' he said with one of his 'devil on steroids' grins that had every female at the tables sighing into their wine glasses as he took his seat.

Introductions were made and Tilda settled back into her seat, her eyes meeting Ezio's across the table. He winked. The man was shameless, she decided, but he had helped her out—which didn't mean she wasn't going to kill him later… Her lids lowered, hiding the gleam there as she added silently, *or something?*

* * *

Ezio sat back, feeling very much a passenger and quite enjoying the experience as he watched his wife charm the table.

Men watched her and envied him. Women envied her a little, but responded to her natural warmth and the fact that her interest in what they said was utterly unfeigned.

She was the genuine article in a room of imitations. She shone and he felt...*proud?*

He had very little interaction with Saul until they were about to leave. The older man leaned in and said quietly, 'I know I offended Tilda, but I hope she has forgiven me and she enjoyed the flowers? Oh, and tell her that I've had a word with Murphy, and he is really interested in her idea.'

'That wasn't too bad.'

'Belt up.' Ezio backed up until he heard the car's warning bleep. 'You were the star turn and everyone there, including me, knew it.'

'Don't be stupid!'

'There you go with rejecting those compliments again... What I want to know is, how did Saul offend you? And how do you know Doyle Murphy?'

'Offend...? Oh... He phoned and, well, he sent me some flowers, and I phoned to thank him but he was fishing, and he asked me if I minded that you slept around and I... I said you didn't, or wouldn't. I had my fingers crossed, but I must have been good, because he apologised. I always knew you'd, well, not be celibate, but I just never thought you'd not be celibate with me.'

'And you are OK with that?'

'You know I'm very OK with that, Ezio, and I don't need any warnings. I know this is just sex.' Sadly, for him it would never be more. He was the wrong man for her, she knew that, but being with him felt so right.

Aware that the dissatisfaction that settled over him was an irrational response to her pragmatic little statement, he drove on in silence for a few minutes.

'And Murphy?' The Irish former racing driver turned entrepreneur was not someone he had ever worked with.

'You read his autobiography…? He cared for his mum who had cancer, and his three brothers and sisters, so Saul thought… I asked Saul for some advice. I thought I might start a charity that would help…'

He listened to her animatedly explain the ideas that were literally bubbling up in her.

'So you went to Saul?'

'He is on the boards of several charities and—'

'So am I.'

'You were busy and I…well…in six months' time I am going to have money and not much to do. I can hardly go back to work for you, can I?'

He said nothing, unwilling to own even to himself that the idea that *somehow* she would remain in his life was even in his head. 'So you have been planning ahead.' For a life without him.

His life would be without Tilda… The bleak, dark future seemed to stretch out into the distance.

'So do you think it's good idea?'

He fought the infinitely childish impulse to retort *would it matter what he thought,* and nodded. 'I think anything you do will be successful and if you need any help, which obviously seems doubtful, let me know.'

'There he is!' Tilda bounced in her seat when she saw her brother, who was talking to an older boy. When he caught sight of them he waved, said something to the other boy, who laughed, then jogged across to where they had parked.

'How was it?'

'It was…' Sam began deadpan then he grinned. 'Amazing!'

The tension left her shoulders as she sagged in relief.

'Tell us about it.'

After five minutes, she was really regretting asking the question.

She took advantage of a lull by inserting, 'Maybe I should have asked you what you didn't like about it.'

'Nothing, only…'

Tilda twisted round in her seat. 'What?'

'The thing is, nearly everyone boards, and if

you're going to be in the chess club and other stuff, well, the day boys miss out on a lot.'

It took a few seconds, but when she processed what he meant she was shocked. 'You want to board?'

'I'd be home every weekend.'

Ezio glanced at Tilda's face. 'How about we discuss this later?'

Sam went straight to the pool the moment they arrived back. From where she sat with Ezio under the shade of a group of lemon trees, she could hear him splashing. She nodded her thanks to the housekeeper as Sybil set down a tray of iced tea.

'I can't believe he wants to board.'

'But you're going let him?'

'It feels like if I was enough…a better…he wouldn't want to go. He's always been… You think I smother him, don't you? You think this will be good for him.'

'Is that what you think?'

She nodded. 'I suppose so,' she admitted with a rueful shrug. 'I'm going to have to let him go, aren't I?'

'You don't have to, but I think you will, because you always put Sam ahead of yourself.'

Before she could respond, Sam appeared dripping with a phone in his hand.

'You two are trending!'

'Don't be stupid,' Tilda said.

'No, *really!*' he insisted, waving the phone while dripping on Tilda's shoes.

'He's right,' Ezio said quietly.

'Let me see,' she snapped, holding out her hand to Sam for the phone.

The image on the screen made her freeze in shock. The blossoms floating around them and the shaft of light filtering through the trees gave the photo an other-worldly quality. Her face was between Ezio's hands and they were kissing. They looked like two people in love, but Tilda knew that this description only applied to one...

She was in love with him and always had been. It was like suddenly noticing an oak tree growing in the middle of her living room: it had always been there; she'd just been walking around it.

'Watch it!' Sam warned, rescuing his phone from her limp grasp. 'That's my life there,' he reproached, jogging back in the direction of the pool.

'You have gone very quiet.'

'You knew?'

'Jake sent it to me, yes.'

'And you didn't think to tell me?'

'It's a good photo, Tilda.'

'Yes, Jake is very good.' *And I am an idiot.*

'He never did take the photo *with* your glasses. I've noticed you have not been wearing them. Have you mislaid them?'

Her green eyes flicked guiltily from side to side but, before she could decide whether to lie or tell the truth about her need for glasses, Sam appeared like a whirlwind and grabbed the towel he had left crumpled on the floor.

'It's OK, she doesn't really need them, it's to make her look older and make bosses take her seriously,' he informed them cheekily.

Ezio waited until Sam had vanished before speaking. 'Is that true?'

She shrugged and found herself wishing that she had her glasses to hide behind.

'So they were props! It's no big thing. I looked young.'

'You are young.' Had she really thought the glasses made her look older? He felt a surge of anger that she'd even felt the need to change her behaviour for her bosses.

'As I said, I looked younger than I am, and it's hard to be taken seriously. I got used to them, they made me feel more confident, and now... I don't need them.' The realisation made her smile.

'I can see that,' he said, looking at the lovely warm woman smiling at him.

'I thought I might work from here for a few days,' he threw out casually, and watched the initial surprise on her face morph into a guarded expression. 'If there are any issues with Sam, I should be here.' It was an explanation about the emotions he was wrestling with he could accept. It made total sense when he factored in that, by the time Sam was settled, this thing would have burnt itself out and he could step back into his life pre-Tilda.

It was a totally logical decision.

'Do you think there will be issues?' she said sharply.

'No, but if there is you might need someone to blame, and it will rather defeat the object of this exercise if I leave my bride before the honeymoon is over. Saul is a man of his generation and very traditional.'

Was it traditional to marry four...five times? she wondered as her shoulders slumped. 'Do you think he has spies planted?' she sniped, gnawing delicately at her full lower lip and drawing his eyes to the lush outline. 'Sorry; I used up all my sparkling charm at lunch. My face was aching with smiling. And when I don't sleep much, I'm cranky.' She closed her eyes... *Did I really just say that?*

'Neither did I, but me? I'm hungry.'

She gasped and her eyes flew wide.

'I hope you've used plenty of sunscreen.' The words were innocuous but the expression in his dark eyes was not. Her stomach went into instant free fall and as she squirmed a little in her chair she was painfully aware of the ache between her legs.

'Always—but actually, I tan quite easily. I got my mum's eyes—she was half-Irish—but my dad's colouring.'

He nodded. Even after the short time exposed to the sun her smooth skin was already tinged with a golden glow that made the green of her eyes even more dramatic.

'I noticed,' he said, thinking of the faint demarcation lines hidden under her clothes he had enjoyed discovering last night, and the tasty gold dusting of freckles on her skin dark against the protected, vulnerable pale parts of her slim body.

The image sent a fresh streak of heat through his already aroused body.

The best way to stop this obsessing about sex, or at least sex with one particular woman, was not to deprive himself of it, he decided, privately likening the deprivation to someone who was dieting but could think of nothing else but food.

The logic might not survive scientific scrutiny but Ezio was not feeling scientific; he was feeling the sort of desperation that he had never experienced in his life.

It had always come easy for him. Women had not often refused him, and the possibility of them doing so had not concerned him; the idea of rejection had never bothered him.

And now it did.

He had broken his own rules, and the hell of it was she couldn't wait to do it again. It wasn't her vulnerability that should have put her off-limits, it was the fact that he was *aware* of that vulnerability that made warning lights flash.

'I know you're worried about Sam boarding—'

She cut across him. 'I know you don't want to

play happy families, Ezio, you just want sex…but it just so happens that I do too, so it's all good, isn't it? We don't have to pretend.' If only that were true, she thought with a sigh

'That sounds cold, Tilda.'

'You were pretty cold to your girlfriends.'

'I really don't think they were looking for kindness. They were looking for sex, a headline to help a career, or a chapter in their tell-all biography, and not necessarily in that order.'

His analysis was probably pretty accurate but she also found it chilling. 'But didn't you ever want… *more* than that?'

'Like *love*?'

'How about liking…friendship?'

'If I want friendship, I'll get a dog,' he said, not even believing himself as he looked ahead. Sam would soon be gone, and soon Tilda would be too; she was building her life without him. *It's what you wanted, isn't it?* Ezio mocked the voice in his head.

CHAPTER ELEVEN

HE TOOK THE steps up to his office two at a time, aware as he dialled into the video meeting with the board that the sight of him without a tie was going to raise a few brows. He hadn't had time to change; the traffic getting to the suburb where the parents of Sam's friend lived had been snarled up for miles.

The boys had not noticed. The spontaneous trip away to the mountain cabin and the construction of a very smoky fire seemed to have made them both happy. Sam had been nagging to go and experience '*off-grid* life', as he put it, ever since Ezio had mentioned his trips up there with his grandfather.

He'd been relying on Tilda refusing permission, but rather to his surprise she had given the plan the green light—but then, Tilda had been a little distant this last week. If that distance had extended to their bedroom, he might have suspected she was cooling off, but she wasn't. She was still the most exciting and uninhibited lover he had ever had.

And that was what mattered, wasn't it? The sex

was incredible and she was not clinging…what more could he want? He ought to be actively not wanting more. *More* involved the sort of complications that would turn his life upside down, and his life was just one long complication.

He was constantly dodging and burying his feelings, but they refused to stay buried… He sighed, caught the scent of her perfume in the air and tuned out of the meeting for a full thirty seconds before coming back, like a man coming up for air, with a curse that turned the air blue.

It was a productive meeting *after* he had cut short all the congratulatory remarks that threatened to take up half the allowed time.

'Thank you for your good wishes! Yes, I'm married, yes, it is business as usual—so let's move on, shall we?'

After that, they whipped through the agenda at a speed that seemed to fluster some members, but Ezio didn't see much point hanging around. There were places he'd prefer to be and people…well, *one* person…he'd like to be with.

He knew where she was. Halfway through the meeting, he'd seen the distant figure of his temporary wife on the path that led to the private beach, wearing something long and floaty that he imagined himself removing. His groin was still heavy from the testosterone-charged surge he had been helpless to control.

Helplessness was not normally a feeling he suffered, but there were exceptions. A specific one came to mind, along with an image of him lying helpless while Tilda, her clever little hands and even cleverer mouth slowly seduced him.

He'd married Matilda and he'd got Tilda, and Tilda, with her green eyes and sharp tongue, didn't let him get away with a thing—she challenged him on everything, sometimes he suspected just for the hell of it.

The thought should not have made him smile but it did…she had clearly spent the last four years disapproving of him and now she didn't have to hide it. His little puritan with the hungry eyes… She was a mass of contradictions.

Seeing himself through those eyes was not the most comfortable feeling in the world for someone who didn't care about the opinion of others.

His phone bleeped. It was head of Sam's academy, asking if he'd agree to be involved with a fund raiser, and the hell of it was he heard himself agreeing.

Three weeks married and he had probably reduced the salary of half the hacks on the continent, he decided, self-mockery tugging one corner of his mouth upwards.

Tilda pulled the silk kaftan over her head and laid it on top of the bag containing her towel before she kicked off her flat woven sandals. The sand was hot under foot as she ran down to the water's edge and stood for a few moments, training her senses to the sound of the waves and trying to shut out the chaos in her head.

After taking the pregnancy test, the initial relief had worn off and she was aware of a troubling sadness that she couldn't shake. Obviously *not* being pregnant was a good thing, but there was a small part of her that felt... Oh God, she didn't know how she was feeling—not panic, at least, which was how she'd been feeling all week.

She was just late, not pregnant, and she didn't have to tell Ezio, who was always so incredibly careful with her in that way.

'It's a good thing!' she yelled at the ocean.

But not a happy ending. There could be no happy endings for a woman who had fallen in love with Ezio, she had finally accepted that. She wanted to be the mother to babies Ezio didn't want...not with her, at least.

Unless that woman's idea of happiness was seeing the man she loved lose interest, cheat or move on.

Her chin firmed. It would be hard to feel sympathy for a woman with such self-destructive impulses, she concluded as she waded in deeper until the warm water lapped around her waist before she dove into and under the first wave.

She thought back to how her dad had taught her to swim on their Cornwall summer holidays. His '*water baby mermaid*', he had called her. The water she swam through now bore no resemblance to the icy, toe-numbing Atlantic dips of her childhood. She enjoyed the embrace of the warmth as, head-down, she struck out.

She paused when she reached a point that was not too far out and began to swim parallel to the shore. Coming to the end of an imaginary lane line, she duck-dived, as sleek as a seal, and swam back. The monotony of the action slowly emptied her mind and finally the strength in her legs.

Flipping over onto her back, she lay there, arms spread, just giving the occasional kick to stay afloat. Eyes closed, she could still see the filtered sun overhead through the paper-thin covering of her eyelids, a hazy glow.

It was tempting to stay that way, but she knew the dangers of exposing herself to the midday sun. She flipped back and, treading water, pushed the hanks of saturated hair from her face.

The villa probably didn't have a bad angle, but the view of the white marble walls from this vantage point was pretty spectacular; the modern, sea-facing lower level that led out to the gorgeously groomed terraces and the spectacular infinity pool was probably seen at its best from the ocean.

The only person who had a better view than her at that moment was the person on the small red sailing boat she could see on the horizon. She waved, even though she knew he couldn't see her, and struck out for the shore.

If Ezio had been in his office in the square tower, he'd have been able to see her. The thought made her lose her rhythm and go under. Swallowing a mouth-ful of salt water, she surfaced, coughing. If she was honest with herself, the reason she often chose the sea for her swim in preference to the infinity pool was the excellent view of it Ezio had from his eyrie. She liked the idea of him watching her. She loved the idea of him not being able to take his eyes off her...*while it lasted.*

No, she would not go there. She was determined to extract every last second of pleasure from being with him, and she already had a lot of memories stored away to look back on and probably cry over later.

By the time she walked out of the shallows, her legs were shaking. She was reflecting on her levels of fitness, or at least lack of them, as she walked up the sand to the spot where she had left her bag. She gath-ered her hair in her fist and, deftly twisting it into a rope, squeezed out some of the excess moisture.

Dropping on her knees beside the towel, she slung her hair back and automatically tightened the clip, holding one earring in and then going to the other.

'Oh, God!' she cried, desperately patting her bare ear as though it could materialise.

From where he stood watching, at the point where the cypress trees met the sand, Ezio watched her increasingly frenzied fingertip-search of the imme-diate area.

By the time he reached her she was walking, head

bent, trying to follow her own footprints in the sand
that were fast disappearing as it dried.

'What is wrong?'

She straightened on the sea edge and spun round.
Ezio was standing there looking gorgeous. She felt
a surge of irrational relief, as if him just being there
could make things all right.

She watched as a sudden breeze caused the
strands of well-cut dark hair to blow flat against his
skull, and the hem of the black T-shirt he was wearing flutter and lift, revealing a slice of flat brown
belly. Then, as the wind direction shifted, it was
pulled tight against his body, revealing the sinewy
strength of his powerful shoulders. Had she wanted
to trace the corrugated ridge of muscles across his
washboard-flat belly, she could have.

The initial weird flutter of misplaced relief when
she'd seen him was swiftly replaced by a much more
sane dismay. She had lost her earring!

'What are you doing here?'

His hooded eyes moved in a slow sweep up her
body, from her feet to her face.

'Have you lost something?'

'Yes.'

'Are you going to tell me what?'

'Just being a bit of a drama queen is all,' she said,
not quite meeting his eyes.

'You are many things but not a drama queen.'

He watched as she blinked to clear the tears that

pooled in her emerald eyes, biting down hard on her quivering lip.

'I lost it,' she croaked out.

Her distress touched him in a part of his heart he'd thought was dead. He walked across and placed his hands on her shoulders, aware of the warm smoothness of her skin as she continued to shiver violently as he pulled her into his body.

'Calm down…look at me!' he said, cupping a hand under her chin and gently turning her tear-stained, tragic face up to his. Something tightened in his chest as he studied the purity of her features. 'Good…now, lost what?'

He could see the muscles in her throat work overtime to contain a sob that was fighting to escape. 'My earring.'

'Your mother's earring,' he realised, pulling her in tight against him.

'Yeah—stupid, I know.' She gulped. 'Not like it's worth a million dollars.'

'It's worth more to you.' His hands slid down her arms and, as he pushed her away from him and looked down into her face, he felt something kick hard in his chest.

He had never embarked on any project without weighing all possible outcomes, but he really hadn't seen this one coming, recognising the swell of protective tenderness for what it was. So much for his *perfect* solution—'no down side' he'd told himself, beyond the fact that he'd be losing the best PA he'd ever had.

There were other PAs, he'd told himself.

There was no other Tilda.

A fresh wave of heat seared through his already aroused body as his eyes slid over her slim figure, the black Lycra concealing enough to excite the imagination and revealing enough to entice the senses. The stark black was the perfect foil to her pale gold-tinged skin, and the swimsuit itself cut high on the thigh emphasised the slim length of her slender legs. It clung to her narrow ribcage and narrow waist, showed off the delicate, carved perfection of her collar bones and displayed her tight, high, perfect small breasts.

She'd hidden all that, but it wasn't just her physicality she had been concealing. His PA had always had a mind and an opinion of her own but she no longer felt the need to be subtle.

'It's just, I don't have much left that was Mum's. She didn't have much jewellery, but the rest... While we were at the funeral someone broke into the house and took it.'

She lifted her head as Ezio released a string of curses. He looked pretty awesome mad, and he was mad at that moment.

'I know,' she said when he paused for breath. 'Utter callous bastards... Apparently they had quite a thing going—they read the funeral notices and knew when the house would be empty.'

'They were caught?' Ezio asked grimly.

She nodded. 'Yes, but not much was recovered, which is why...' She twirled the remaining earring, a gold stud with a small baroque pearl-drop. 'Ah, well, it is what it is...' She attempted a chuckle, fell short and produced something approaching a strangled croak. 'I must have looked crazy, crawling around like that! My own fault for wearing them, really. I should have kept them safe, but Mum always said, what was the point saving things for "best"?'

As she sketched inverted commas in the air, she realised that the concept probably meant nothing to him. Pretty things, like pretty women, were all disposable to him. What did he hold precious? she wondered.

'You mother sounds like she had a healthy outlook on life.'

A slow, reflective smile lit up her face. Lost in the memories, she didn't notice his sharp intake of breath.

'She did. Mum was always a "glass half-full" person, and she'd have said it is just a thing...things don't make you happy.' Her slender shoulders lifted in a shrug. 'It's gone,' she said, sounding a lot more philosophical than she felt. 'I could have lost it absolutely anywhere...probably when I was swimming.'

'You're a little mermaid.'

He watched her eyes fill with tears. 'What...did something happen on your trip to Athens?'

Nothing, except I know I'm not carrying your

baby. She had convinced herself, and she'd been so convinced that when the test had come up negative she had repeated it twice before she believed the results—not pregnant, just late.

The tears began to leak and she brushed them away. 'No, it's just my dad used to call me that… Oh, hell, I don't know what's wrong with me.' She did—she loved him.

'Oh, Tilda, I'm sorry.'

'Heavens…' She sniffed. 'You have no need to be sorry, you're just—' She closed her mouth over the 'perfect' she had been about to say and belatedly became aware that the thin wet Lycra of her swimsuit offered very little concealment of her nipples, which had sprouted to pebble-hard prominence. She half-lifted her arms to cover herself, before the utter ridiculousness of her self-consciousness hit her.

This was a man who had seen and explored every inch of her body.

'What…?' She watched as he kicked off his shoes.

'What are you doing? You're wearing your clothes…'

'If I find your earring—'

'That's not possible…it could be anywhere.'

'You have freckles,' he said, brushing a finger across the gold-tinted skin of her nose. 'If I find it you owe me…'

'Owe you what?' He already had her heart and soul; there wasn't a hell of a lot left, she thought dismally.

His wicked grin glimmered on his bronze face. 'Oh, I'll think of something.'

Standing on the shore, a hand shading her eyes, she watched as he waded in until the water was chest-deep before he dived under. He was down so long that she had actually started to wade in herself when he reappeared, his dark hair saturated. He raised a hand and dived straight back under.

It was a process that he repeated, and actually she lost count. She had called out for him to stop several times but, if he'd heard her, he'd ignored her.

She was contemplating swimming out to him to put a stop to this craziness when he reappeared but didn't go back down. Instead, he struck out strongly for the shore.

He stood up and started to wade towards her, making her think of some sea god rising from the waves. Then as he got closer she saw the glint of something in his hand.

She jumped up and down in the shallows.

'I don't believe it! I don't believe it.'

She waded out to meet him and snatched the earring from his fingers. He caught her by the waist and swung her around.

Held high above him, she curved down and took his face between her hands, raining kisses on his wet brown face. 'Oh, thank you. I have no idea how… It was impossible… Oh, you beautiful man, I *love* you!' The laughter faded from his face. 'Not literally, obviously.'

The look vanished but she sensed caution in his eyes as he planted her back on her feet. Together they walked up the sand and reached where her possessions lay. Tilda went to bend to retrieve them and stopped as she felt his hands on her breasts, cupping and kneading them through the fabric as he stepped in close, allowing her to feel the full strength of his arousal as he pressed into her back as his thumbs traced the bold projection of her aching nipples.

Her back arched as he continued to massage her breasts and slide his tongue up the length of her exposed neck. He turned her round and she lifted her passion-glazed eyes to his face, mesmerised by the mask of primitive need she saw. He looked almost in pain as he took the earring from her fingers and with elaborate care put it back in her earlobe, leaving behind a million whispering, silken threads of painful sensation.

'It's a miracle.'

'I think you're a miracle,' he rasped, and her heartbeat escalated.

He kissed her then, not fiercely, but with deep, drugging kisses that left her feeling limp and languid. Dizzying desire swirled through her as he picked her up and carried her up the beach to where the pines met the sand. There he laid her down gently in the shade.

He knelt there, drinking her in before he slowly slid the straps of her swimsuit down her shoulders. A few seconds later, she was naked.

'You're beautiful.'

'So are you,' she whispered back, watching through closed eyelids as he stripped off his tee shirt, pulling it over his head to reveal the sleek, hard muscles of his torso. A moment later his wet jeans were gone too.

Just looking at him, standing there shamelessly aroused, took her to the brink.

Ezio brought her back to that place several times as he spent time moving down her body, touching her everywhere, his mouth and fingers finding secret places and nerve-endings where she hadn't known they existed.

When he did slide between her parted legs, his kisses tasted of her.

'*Theos*, you are so tight and wet,' he groaned, moving slowly until, urged on by her cries, the urgency pumping through him, he thrust in hard, continuing the carnal onslaught until her muscles tightened around him and he let himself go.

It wasn't until a few moments later as their sweat-slicked bodies lay entwined that he realised what he had done.

Tilda sensed his withdrawal.

She rolled on her stomach to look at his face.

'I'm sorry,' he said, self-recrimination written into the drawn lines of his face.

'What for?' He was about to tell he'd slept with someone… She was so convinced that when he did explain, despite the seriousness, she almost laughed.

'I didn't use protection. It was…there is not much point saying sorry, is there?'

Tilda pulled herself up into a sitting position.

'It happened, and I am at least partly to blame, but, well…' she said, 'really, it isn't *that* time of my cycle… Well, actually, I'm already really very late, so the likelihood is not zero but low. You might have noticed that I've been—'

'I noticed.'

'That's why I went into Athens today—not for retail therapy. I bought a test and it was negative. I'm not pregnant, so you can relax, and as for the future, well…'

He cut across her. 'But you thought you were?'

'I was a bit worried,' she admitted. 'Though you've always been very…considerate.'

'Not today I wasn't.'

'No, well, I suppose these things happen.'

He was suddenly on his feet, dragging on his clothes. 'Not to me they don't!'

An icy stone inside her chest, Tilda jumped to her feet and began to pull on her wet swimsuit. She had got the fabric as far as her waist when he turned around. His eyes dropped to the coral-tipped peaks of her breasts before he turned away, murmuring something under his breath.

'Are you going to tell me what is going on here, Ezio?'

He turned back and she couldn't believe that this

was the same man who had made love to her so tenderly a few minutes ago. His face was like stone.

'I'm not pregnant.'

'But if you were it would be my fault. You're right—it could happen again. I don't want that responsibility. I am not father material. I'm too selfish…too flawed.' About the only thing in his favour, the only thing that made him better than his own father, was the fact he didn't want to hurt her.

Her relief had highlighted his disappointment at the fact that he had tried to bury for so long—that a part of him craved family, connection, all the things he poured scorn on. Now the irony was *she* didn't want those things either when all he could see was her body growing big with his child. 'All of this is a result of, well, *proximity*. You were there and… Honestly, this is an exercise in futility,' he said. 'You think it's going some place, but it isn't.'

'You're not your father, and I'm not that woman who broke your heart. I wouldn't do that to you, Ezio.'

But I'd do it to you, he thought, bitter self-revulsion showing in his eyes as he delivered his cruel-to-be-kind killer blow. 'I loved *her*, Tilda.'

She reacted as if he'd struck her, but it was the only way he could think of to push her far enough away for him to save her or himself.

'So this…!' She gestured down at the hollow they had created on the ground, cold now, but moments ago warm from their body heat. 'It was just a technical exercise, no heart, no emotion. I don't believe that… What scares you so much about emotions, Ezio?'

She turned and fled then, not caring how she looked, just not caring about anything. Like a wounded animal, she locked herself in her room and cried… It was dark outside when she stopped.

And her mind was set.

She packed her bags, washed her face and went to find Ezio.

'I'll leave in the morning.'

He looked up from the blank computer screen. 'That is not necessary. I am flying back to London tomorrow.'

'Fine, but I'm not staying here.' Where everywhere would remind her of their short, doomed affair. The idea filled her with horror. 'I'm going to see Sam in the morning. I want to tell him in person what's happening. I'll find somewhere nice near the school. Will you say goodbye to him?'

CHAPTER TWELVE

THE TOP-FLOOR APARTMENT was too big for one, but when Sam came home at the weekend she'd be glad of the space. The pool in the basement had sold it to her, and she'd tried to sell it to Sam without much success.

Knowing he was anxious about her reaction, she had struggled to hide her hurt when he'd expressed his wish to spend a few weekends with Ezio at the villa.

'Isn't that what happens to kids when their parents divorce?'

'This is different. Ezio is not your parent, Sam.'

'Neither are you,' had been his hurtful but totally logical response.

She just hoped that he'd get used to it in time.

She was piling some laundry into the washing machine when there was a buzz at the door.

She pressed the button that connected her to the keyed entry lobby.

'It's Ezio. We need to talk.'

'No, there is nothing—'

'It's Sam.'

She buzzed him up and waited for the knock on the door. When it came, she took a deep breath, painted what she hoped was cold neutrality on her face and opened the door, stepping back before his imposing presence appeared in her hallway.

He didn't waste time on small talk. 'Sam is missing.'

She felt her knees give and grabbed a nearby chair. 'What do you mean? How do you know this and I don't?'

'When you changed your number, presumably to block me, you failed to give the school your new number.'

'Oh, God…missing as in…?'

'As in gone from his room. Nobody knows where he is. The school contacted me when they couldn't get hold of you…the kids are searching the school grounds and buildings. They're holding off on calling the police.'

Her hand went to her mouth and panic slid through her like ice. Her brain froze all she could feel was fear. 'This is my fault! I brought him here, let him think we were a family and— Oh, my God! What am I going to do? We need to call the police! Why is no one calling the police?'

His hands went to her shoulders. 'You are going to breathe and then you are going to come with me… I think I might know where he is.'

'Then why aren't you there, finding him?' she exploded, pushing his hands away.

'Because I thought you might like to come along.'

A frown of instant contrition crossed her pale face. 'Of course you did. I'm sorry.' She flicked a conciliatory look at his face, noticing the pronounced edges of his cheek bones and some interesting shadows under his dark, intense eyes. 'It's just when I think—'

'Do not think,' he ordered calmly. 'There is little point torturing yourself with imagined scenarios while Sam is probably right now sitting in the cabin, living off the land.'

'Living off the land?'

'You know, back to nature and whittling… I happened to mention that I ran away there once.'

He closed his eyes, waiting for her wrath, but all he got was a squeeze of his arm.

'Oh, God, I can't tell you how… That's marvellous!' She beamed. 'What are we waiting for?'

He nodded down at her feet.

'Oh, yes.' She ran across the room, shoved her feet in a pair of sandals and was at the door before him.

She struggled to protect her hair form the updraft from the helicopter as it landed.

'Right!' he yelled over the din. 'You get that this can only take us to the…well about a mile off the cabin? But the forester leaves a four-wheel drive in the shed there and he'd left the keys in the ignition for us.'

She nodded and ducked her head as she ran behind him.

Inside she put on the mufflers and sat silently trying not to allow the lurid scenarios in her head to take root. A few minutes in, she became aware of the conversation between Ezio and the pilot.

'Will the rain storm stop us landing?'

Ezio shook his head and spoke into his ear piece. 'No problem,' he said, seeing no point in adding that the road to the cabin might be more of a problem, and taking comfort from the fact that the last time it had been washed out was ten years ago.

By the time they landed, the rain was falling horizontally. She had imagined Greece to be a dry place; she'd not seen anything this bad since she and Sam had tried camping in the Lake District.

'What if we don't find him?'

'We will, and you're not going fall apart.'

She looked up at him and smiled. 'No, I'm not, I'm a little trooper,' she mocked.

'No, you're a wonder of a woman,' he contradicted her, before immediately transferring his attention to the map on his phone. 'The four-wheel drive should be fifty yards that way,' he said when they landed.

It was.

'Right, this might be a bit bumpy.'

She flashed him a tense grin. 'Don't worry about me!'

Theos, but he did; the self-denial seemed futile

at the point when he would have walked through a sea of sharks to protect her, and any attempt on his part to deny the fact was by that point redundant.

'Right, *yineka mou*, hold tight.'

Tilda did. The white-knuckle ride lasted what seemed like an age but was probably in reality less than fifteen minutes. At times it seemed as if they were driving along a river bed and there had been some drops that she coped with by simply closing her eyes.

Finally, the cabin came into view—a lot less primitive than it had seemed in her mind.

'There are no lights,' she observed fearfully. It might be the afternoon but the storm had turned the sky night-dark.

'There is no electricity,' he told her as he pulled up in the gravelled parking area that was now a small pond.

She clambered out before he come to help her, landing up to her ankles in water. She sensed him at her side as she ran up to the front door.

Calling her brother's name, she rushed in, pausing as behind her she heard the hiss of flame as Ezio lit a lantern.

'He's not here!'

But something was… She watched as Ezio went across to the table where there stood a large bunch of red roses and a champagne bottle inside an ice bucket, against which was propped a note.

Ezio held it up, his eyes scanning the single page of writing.

'I think you need to read this,' he said, handing it to Tilda.

Dear both,

Ezio is not so stupid so I'm assuming you found this... I just thought you needed a bit of wake-up call. I don't know much, but I do know you are both crazy about each other. So get real, guys, kiss and make up. I don't want to be the kid from a broken home.

Theo's mum and dad are away, so he gave me the house keys. I'll head back to school for double physics.

Oh, and by the way, I didn't shoplift it, Tilda. Theo's mum bought the champagne for me. She thought I wanted to buy you two a present. She thinks I'm very sweet. Also, it cost an arm and a leg, so you owe me.

Love, Sam

By the time she had finished, the tears were pouring down Tilda's cheeks. 'I will kill him stone-dead.'

'Not if I get there before you. Manipulated by a fourteen-year-old. It makes you wonder how scary he is going to be in ten years' time.'

'I'm so sorry.'

'It's OK. That's what family is for, or so I understand.' Heart beating fast, she stared up at him, not daring to believe… Saying nothing, she locked her eyes on his, not able to believe that anything she could say could bridge the gap that he had built over years of isolating himself.

'Have you moved on, Tilda?'

She shook her head. 'I'm a work in progress.' She sniffed.

'Your brother is right. I am crazy about you, Tilda. I can't believe it took a fourteen-year-old, even if he is a genius, to bring me to my senses. I have never in my life felt about any woman the way I do you… It terrified me…the thought of hurting you *terrified* me… The thought of being a bad father terrifies me still. I couldn't protect my mother, but I thought by pushing you away I could protect you.' He took her chin in his fingers and with his thumb brushed away the tears running down her face.

'I spent a day sitting there, feeling noble and self-sacrificing, then I spent the next day trying to figure out how to get you back. I am such a coward… I was scared of giving you the power to hurt me.'

He moved in closer, taking both her hands in his and raising them to his lips. 'But, Tilda Raven, I give you my heart—it is yours, and you have the power to crush it in your little hand. I want a real marriage. I want a real wife…a family.'

She fell into his kiss, tears streaming down her face. 'I love you so much…it hurts,' she said, pressing a hand to her chest.

'You know that I will never betray you…' He

could say that finally, knowing it was true that Tilda was the love of his life.

'I trust you, Ezio, with my life and my heart.'

'You realise that Sam is going to be very smug,' he said, stroking her cheek lovingly.

'Shall we pretend to hate one another?'

Ezio shook his head, his expression darkening. 'I have had enough pretending to last me a lifetime. There is some champagne there with our names on it.'

'Afterwards, I think.' Being loved by Ezio would put more fizz in her veins than a crate of champagne.

She sighed her happiness as his lips claimed hers.

EPILOGUE

'I ONLY ASKED for a new laptop…you had no need to go to this much trouble.'

Sam stroked the beard he was trying to grow with limited success as he looked down at the red-headed baby sleeping in the crib. In the past six months he had grown and now topped six feet, gangly but filling out, as he had started training when he'd got on the school swimming team.

'I think it's really handy. Joint birthday parties with Olivia for ever? Balloons and cake…?'

Sam rolled his eyes and tried and failed not to look enchanted as the baby opened her big, dark eyes and wrapped her hand tightly around his finger.

'Wow, my niece is super-strong! Do you suppose she has super-powers?'

'She has a volume super-power,' said Ezio, who walked into the nursery, looking gorgeous, with dark circles of sleep deprivation under his eyes. 'Especially at two o'clock in the morning. You,' he said, walking across to where Tilda was folding tiny baby clothes, 'Should be asleep. Sleep while she sleeps—that's what all the books say.'

Tilda lifted her head to receive the warm and loving kiss before she leaned into his body, laying her head on his chest. Her husband had read *all* the books cover to cover, and had driven her mad trying to wrap her in cotton wool during her pregnancy.

'I just like looking at her. She's so perfect and her hair makes me think of Mum...' They had named their baby daughter—who had arrived a few weeks early, small but perfectly healthy—Olivia after her grandmother.

'Right,' Sam said, extracting his finger from the chubby grip. 'I'll be off, but I'll see you at the weekend.'

'Good luck at the chess tournament,' Tilda said, kissing his cheek; it required her to stand on tip toe.

'I don't need luck, I have skill,' Sam said, polishing his chest and looking disgustingly smug. 'Just make the next one a boy so I have someone to play football with.'

'I'll have you know my daughter will run rings around you on the football pitch.' Ezio reached out with his foot to rock the cradle as sounds of grumpy protests emerged from wriggling, red-faced bundle inside.

'Probably, I am pretty awful... See you...' He strolled off just as the baby let out a loud squeal.

'I've noticed that Sam always manages to leave just as Olivia starts to yell!' Tilda observed, expertly scooping the baby out of the crib, a tired, happy glow in her face as she stared down at their daughter.

'He's a genius, that boy.' Ezio came to stand behind Tilda, who laid her head on his chest. 'I still have nightmares about that drive to the hospital.' He sighed. 'I actually forgot how to start a car.'

Tilda tilted her head and smiled up at him. 'You remembered, that was what counted, and I got there on time.'

'Just,' Ezio recalled with feeling. 'You might have mentioned you were in labour two hours earlier.'

'Well, I wasn't due, and it was in the middle of the fund raiser.' Her charity had gone from strength to strength over the past year, but she was taking maternity leave from what had become a pretty full-on commitment. 'I thought it might be Braxton Hicks.'

'Well, it was no practice, it was the real thing... very real... Oh, God, Tilda, you were brilliant, you know that? I could never do what you did.'

'Well, darling, you really don't have the right equipment. But the equipment you do have...' she added with a saucy grin as her eyes dropped down his body '...is pretty much perfect. Is she asleep or...?'

'Put her down,' Ezio whispered. As much as he loved their baby, the moments he had his beautiful wife alone to himself were rare enough not to be wasted.

As they carefully laid her down and went on tip

toe from the room, there was a loud explosion of angry baby sobs.

Ezio sighed and happily kissed his wife. They had the rest of their lives to be together.

Together but never alone.

* * * * *

If you couldn't put
Claimed by Her Greek Boss *down,*
then why not try these other stories
by Kim Lawrence?

The Spaniard's Surprise Love-Child
Claiming His Unknown Son
Waking Up in His Royal Bed
The Italian's Bride on Paper
Innocent in the Sicilian's Palazzo

Available now!

WE HOPE YOU ENJOYED
THIS BOOK FROM
H HARLEQUIN
PRESENTS

Escape to exotic locations where passion knows no bounds.

Welcome to the glamorous lives of royals and billionaires, where passion knows no bounds. Be swept into a world of luxury, wealth and exotic locations.

8 NEW BOOKS AVAILABLE EVERY MONTH!

#4049 HER CHRISTMAS BABY CONFESSION
Secrets of the Monterosso Throne
by Sharon Kendrick
Accepting a flight home from a royal wedding with Greek playboy Xanthos is totally out of character for Bianca. Yet when they're suddenly snowbound together, Bianca chooses to embrace their deliciously dangerous chemistry, just once...only to find herself carrying a shocking secret!

#4050 A WEEK WITH THE FORBIDDEN GREEK
by Cathy Williams
Grace Brown doesn't have time to fantasize about her boss, Nico Doukas...never mind how attractive he is! But when she accompanies him on a business trip, the earth-shattering desire between them makes keeping things professional impossible...

#4051 THE PRINCE'S PREGNANT SECRETARY
The Van Ambrose Royals
by Emmy Grayson
Clara is shocked to discover she's carrying her royal boss's baby! The last thing she wants is to become Prince Alaric's convenient princess, but marriage will protect their child from scandal. Can their honeymoon remind them that more than duty binds them?

#4052 RECLAIMING HIS RUNAWAY CINDERELLA
by Annie West
After years of searching for the heiress who fled just hours after their convenient marriage, Cesare finally tracks Ida down. Intent on finalizing their divorce, he hadn't counted on the undeniable attraction between them! Dare they indulge in the wedding night they never had?

#4053 NINE MONTHS AFTER THAT NIGHT
Weddings Worth Billions
by Melanie Milburne

Billionaire hotelier Jack is blindsided when he discovers the woman he spent one mind-blowing night with is in the hospital... having his baby! Marriage is the only way to make sure his daughter has the perfect upbringing. But only *if* Harper accepts his proposal...

#4054 UNWRAPPING HIS NEW YORK INNOCENT
Billion-Dollar Christmas Confessions
by Heidi Rice

Alex Costa doesn't trust *anyone.* Yet he cannot deny the attraction when he meets sweet, innocent Ellie. Keeping her at arm's length could prove impossible when the fling they embark on unwraps the most intimate of secrets...

#4055 SNOWBOUND IN HER BOSS'S BED
by Marcella Bell

When Miriam is summoned to Benjamin Silver's luxurious Aspen chalet, she certainly doesn't expect a blizzard to leave her stranded there for Hanukkah! Until the storm passes, she must battle her scandalous and ever-intensifying attraction to her boss...

#4056 THEIR DUBAI MARRIAGE MAKEOVER
by Louise Fuller

Omar refuses to allow Delphi to walk away from him. His relentless drive has pushed her away and now he must convince her to return to Dubai to save their marriage. But is he ready to reimagine everything he believed their life together would be?

YOU CAN FIND MORE INFORMATION ON UPCOMING HARLEQUIN TITLES, FREE EXCERPTS AND MORE AT HARLEQUIN.COM.

HPCNMRB0922

SPECIAL EXCERPT FROM

(H) HARLEQUIN

PRESENTS

*Cesare intends to finalize his divorce to his runaway
bride, Ida. Yet he hadn't counted on discovering Ida's
total innocence in their marriage sham. Or on the
attraction that rises swift and hot between them...
Dare they indulge in the wedding night they never had?*

*Read on for a sneak preview of
Annie West's 50th book for Harlequin Presents,*
Reclaiming His Runaway Cinderella

"Okay. We're alone. Why did you come looking for me?"

"I thought that was obvious."

How could Ida have forgotten the intensity of that
brooding stare? Cesare's eyes bored into hers as if seeking
out misdemeanors or weaknesses.

But she'd done him no wrong. She didn't owe him
anything and refused to be cowed by that flinty gaze. Ida
shoved her hands deep in her raincoat pockets and raised
her eyebrows.

"It's been a long day, Cesare. I'm not in the mood for
guessing games. Just tell me. What do you want?"

He crossed the space between them in a couple of deceptively easy strides. Deceptive because his expression told her it was the prowl of a predator.

"To sort out our divorce, of course."

"We're still married?"

Don't miss
Reclaiming His Runaway Cinderella
available November 2022 wherever
Harlequin Presents books and ebooks are sold.

Harlequin.com